# *Curious Tales of Bedford Landing*
**A NOVEL**

Susan DuVall

Copyright © 2024 Matisse Fictionary LLC

All rights reserved. No part of this book may be reproduced in any form or by any electronic or mechanical means including information storage and retrieval systems without permission in writing from the author. The only exception is by a reviewer, who may quote short excerpts in a review.

This is a work of fiction. Names, characters, businesses, places, events, locales, and incidents are either the products of the author's imagination or used in a fictitious manner.

ISBN Paperback: 979-8-9905148-0-5
ISBN eBook: 979-8-9905148-1-2

Printed in the United States of America

Book Cover and Interior Design: Creative Publishing Book Design
Cover Illustration: Gabriel Jensen
Interior Art Illustrations: Suzanne Maria Hackett
Editor and Consultant: K.J. Wetherholt

# Part One
# Cult on the Kentucky River

# Contents

| | |
|---|---|
| Bedford Landing Restored | 5 |
| The Bedford Landing Inn | 9 |
| Matt Conway, Investigative Reporter | 15 |
| Bertha Roins Plans Her Move | 19 |
| The Death of John Roins | 21 |
| Bertha Roins Explores Bedford Landing | 25 |
| Sunday at Bedford Landing | 31 |
| Matt Conway Investigation | 37 |
| Audrey Wilcox Disturbing Day | 43 |
| Midnight Misadventure | 51 |
| Bertha Roins Application | 55 |
| Bertha Roins Abysmal Rejection | 61 |
| The Reckoning | 63 |
| Kidnapping of Kaylene Butler | 67 |
| A Discovery in Bertha Roins Room | 71 |
| Rescue at Waveland State Historic Site | 75 |
| Butler Appreciation Day | 81 |

# Bedford Landing Restored

Bedford Landing was a proud, old Kentucky town with a rich history. Over time, the town grew a little worn and ragged around the edges. The population dwindled as young folk moved away for greater opportunities. All that changed five years ago when Amy and Clayton Butler began production of a new television series *Restore My Old House*. As the popularity of the show soared, Bedford Landing saw an influx of adoring fans and with them considerable revenue. Now the courthouse square was freshly landscaped and the surrounding storefronts brightly painted. Along with the fans and television crew came questionable strangers. Among some residents there was a vague sense of disquietude. Yet, as the town prospered, signs of impending darkness were simply ignored.

Success came as a surprise to Clayton and Amy Butler. Both came from generations of tenant farmers. They had married in their teens, and neither had travelled beyond Bedford Landing except for the one high school visit to Frankfort to see the capital. Clayton discovered he had a talent for home repair and began to find odd jobs around town. Soon he became well regarded. To help make ends meet, Amy

Susan DuVall

# Bedford County Courthouse

worked at the local paint store where she spent a lot of time perusing home design magazines. Her grandmother looked after their baby daughter, Kaylene.

Then one day Clayton was approached by his pastor. "Clayton, I've been thinking we need a place to hold Wednesday night prayer suppers and maybe even wedding receptions. That old basement at the church has not been used for years. Why don't you see about fixin' it up?"

Clayton jumped at the opportunity and completed the work with a small budget in three months. Amy helped, adding her own décor touches learned from the home design magazines. So thrilled with the results, the congregation nominated the Butlers to appear as contestants in an HTV home decorating competition. The Butlers easily won. Their audience ratings were highly favorable, and the network decided to take a chance on the Butlers of Bedford Landing. Within months production began on their own show *Restore My Old House*. It was an immediate success. Clayton, Amy, and little Kaylene were adored by the audience for their humility and small-town charm.

To the network's delight, Clayton had a comic streak that played well on *Restore My Old House*. The Butlers learned to leverage it when they made guest appearances on network morning shows and some late night as well. Amy was always careful to steer the conversation around to their commitment to the sanctity of family. She would say. "You know our motto. *Every child deserves to be cherished.*"

The Butlers had little experience running a business, but with the help of outside investors, they diversified into farming, real estate, and online sales. The online sales offered local arts and crafts featured on *Restore My Old House*. Their signature item was a pricey black denim jacket with hand encrusted turquoise. Soon popularized by celebrities in the country music industry, jacket sales skyrocketed. As the Butler fortune grew, the town prospered. Bedford Landing had become a tourist destination for viewers of home renovation shows, and the population began growing for the first time in decades. Fans were moving to the town of their dreams—a town viewed on television by millions.

To express gratitude, the Bedford Landing mayor and city council organized Butler Appreciation Day sure to draw tourists. It would be held on the courthouse square the weekend before the Fourth of July. The council formed a committee of prominent citizens to coordinate the event. Initial plans called for a short ceremony. A large welcome banner would be draped across the front of the courthouse. At 10:00 am, the mayor would give a short speech from the bandstand praising the Butlers. This would be followed by a prayer of thanks from the pastor and the singing of "God Bless America" by a church choir. Clayton Butler had arranged vans for a narrated tour of Restoration Trail. The route would start at the courthouse square and make short stops at each house renovated on *Restore My Old House*, including the Butler Farmhouse. The final stop would be downtown at the new Bedford Mercantile owned by the Butlers.

It was mid-June, and the town of Bedford Landing was energized and hopeful. Recent college graduate Audrey Wilcox was optimistic as well. She had arrived two weeks earlier to launch her career in television as the new intern on *Restore My Old House*. No one could have predicted how the events of the next two weeks would upend all the buoyant plans of Bedford Landing and change the course of Audrey's life.

# The Bedford Landing Inn

The Bedford Landing Inn stood a few blocks from the courthouse square. It was a grand Victorian structure with a wraparound porch. Pawpaw and ancient Chestnut trees provided shade. In the back there was a gazebo and well-tended path leading to the Kentucky River. The Inn had been in the Cline family for well over 100 years. Miss Anacelia Cline had run the Inn for the last thirty-five. She was a quiet, elegant woman, always watchful, never married.

It was Sunday night, and the air was warm and heavy. Often in the evening, guests, friends, and neighbors retired to the porch for a little company and conversation under the steady hum of the large fans above. It was a welcoming place with plenty of comfortable wicker chairs, a swing, and two hand-crafted rockers. Ferns and bright pink geraniums hung from the porch rafters.

That evening, Miss Anacelia was resting in her favorite chair with several travel pamphlets on her lap. She was a slender woman wearing a blue linen dress and sandals, her thick, silver hair piled in a loose updo. Seated proudly next to her was Cezanne, her golden long-haired dachshund. From the steps below, Lucas Todd appeared,

holding a bottle of prize Kentucky bourbon. He was a large man with a commanding presence. "Good evening, Miss Anacelia. You look particularly fetching this evening." "Why thank you, Mr. Todd." She watched Lucas with concern as he favored one leg climbing the steps. "Please sit before everyone arrives, I want to show you these pamphlets about Portugal." But there was no time to talk as Judge Hedger Northcutt called from the sidewalk "Good evening, you all. I hear you have some new guests, Miss Anacelia." Hedger was a round, little man who took care to wear his best seersucker pants and fresh cotton shirts in public. Soon others began to gather on the porch.

Lucas Todd and Judge Hedger Northcutt were porch regulars and life-time friends of Miss Anacelia. They had been collaborating on a murder mystery novel for some time. Progress was slow as Judge Northcutt often revised the story. Lucas Todd did not always agree. Their current conundrum was how to introduce early suspense to engage the reader. "I think we should present the unexplained fatalities in Chapter Two," Judge Northcutt proposed firmly. Lucas Todd shook his head and replied. "Not so sure about that, Hedger. If we do that, we detract from the element of surprise in Chapter Four. What do you think, Miss Anacelia?" With kindness and patience Miss Anacelia had agreed to be their editor. However, she was always careful to deflect when there were disagreements. "This is certainly a difficult decision, gentlemen. I know you will come up with the best approach." Miss Anacelia leaned back in her chair and stroked Cezanne.

After the mystery novel discussion slowed, Judge Northcutt turned to Audrey Wilcox, "Miss Wilcox. What can you tell us about the kerfuffle over at the Gibson House on Friday?" Audrey Wilcox was a guest at the Inn and had become a porch regular herself. She recently earned a degree in Film and Television Studies and proudly landed a paid summer internship with *Restore My Old House*. All her life Audrey dreamed of a career in television, and she was convinced this internship was her ticket to success. In her brief time in Bedford Landing, she had become the Inn's resident expert on *Restore My Old House* and was warmly regarded by Miss Anacelia. Audrey was a tall thin girl with short dark hair and a quick, engaging smile. She wore large, framed glasses and could be seen wearing tees and cargo pants most of the time. Always eager to please, Audrey sat up straight and began her account of the zany incident.

"Well, it all started like this. We had just begun the shoot. Mrs. Butler and Kaylene were placing books on the living room shelves, when there was this noise from outside that got louder and louder. Of course, we had to stop production because of the interference with our sound system. I looked through the front window and saw a group of tourists and fans gathered on the sidewalk. They all seemed to be talking at the same time, and this one woman had a very loud, shrill laugh. It was awful. There was no way we could continue filming, so I decided to go out to quiet the crowd. When I opened the door, this middle-aged couple barged into the dining room and knocked over one of the chairs."

"Oh. My goodness," said Miss Anacelia. Audrey turned to Miss Anacelia and continued. "Yeah, it was unbelievable! Without an apology or anything, they moved into the kitchen, and you won't believe this. This woman picks up a large knife and begins laughing while her husband takes photos. It was that same loud, shrill laugh we heard from the crowd." Lucas Todd exclaimed, "This has gotten completely out of hand." Audrey paused a second for dramatic effect. "Within minutes the couple was escorted out of the house. And get this. They were met with cheers from the crowd." Judge Northcutt groaned. Audrey continued. "Someone must have called the Sheriff, because in just a few minutes we heard the siren. Boy, did that crowd move away quickly when the Sheriff's car pulled up." Judge Northcutt said. "We can always count on Sheriff Harlan Yeager." Lucas Todd and Miss Anacelia nodded proudly.

Miss Anacelia said, "Lord, I am sure everyone was glad to have that resolved." Audrey sheepishly answered. "Well not quite. I walked on set to put the dining chair back, tripped on a cord, and knocked over the sound guy's equipment. This meant production was delayed a full hour." She paused briefly and looked anxiously to Miss Anacelia. "Maybe I should have just waited for security guys before opening the door. I sure hope I have a job tomorrow." Lucas Todd had practiced law in Bedford Landing for thirty-five years. He smiled at Audrey. "Tripped over a cord, you say? I would not fret. Seems to me there is a workplace safety issue here. My guess is your internship will last the full summer and you will receive a fine reference." Audrey's taut face began to ease. His kind manner and deep voice had a way of inspiring confidence.

Then with furrowed brow, Lucas Todd turned to Miss Anacelia, "You know there's been a lot of talk in town about all these fans. Folks are calling them 'stalkers and gawkers.' Cannot for the life of me understand how grown men and women behave this way. They are not just a nuisance; they are a menace to our town." As former mayor, Lucas Todd regarded vulgar behavior in his town as a personal insult. Miss Anacelia was equally appalled and slowly shook her head. Audrey saw an opening.

The topic of outrageous, delusional fan behavior was of particular interest to Audrey. Last semester she took a class on parasocial relationships. Adjusting her glasses, she somberly explained to the porch occupants how fans can develop parasocial attachments to celebrities. "A fan can become delusional and imagine a relationship with a celebrity who does not even know the fan exists. In the extreme, their imaginings can develop into obsessive stalking and worse. It is quite similar to erotomania," said Audrey with great authority. When she finished, everyone was silent. Judge Northcutt stood up to stretch his short legs and pronounced, "Well, I don't expect to see any of that here in Bedford Landing. Those folks on Friday probably just got wound up." Miss Anacelia looked skeptical and slipped silently into the parlor.

Conversation on the porch took many turns before Lucas asked, "Has anyone been by the migrant camp out at Butler Farm? What are those kids doing out there?" Before anyone could respond, Miss Anacelia appeared on the porch. "Beg your pardon, Lucas. I would like to introduce our new guests. Please welcome Mrs. Bertha Roins of Cincinnati, Ohio and Mr. Matt Conway of New Haven, Connecticut. While you all get acquainted, who would like an "Old Fashioned" cocktail in honor of our very own Colonel James E. Pepper." Turning to Audrey with a smile, Miss Anacelia said, "Colonel Pepper invented the 'Old Fashioned' cocktail, don't you know." Lucas added, "Colonel Pepper had a thoroughbred farm not far from here." In his semi-retirement, Lucas had taken an interest in Kentucky history.

# Matt Conway, Investigative Reporter

Matt Conway was an investigative reporter. Standing at 5'8" and 145 pounds, Matt had learned to succeed through the force of his own personality and had earned early recognition in his career. After graduation from Yale, Matt was offered a position at a small news outlet in Massachusetts. That same year he was accepted in the coveted Reveal Investigative Fellowship program. With the help of a local girl he was dating, Matt uncovered a school board corruption scheme involving bribery and money laundering. The BBC published his article in a series on the misuse of funds and deterioration of American schools.

His next article involved a small church in Alabama. The pastor had convinced his members to engage in the sacramental offering of their daughters to the pastor on their tenth birthday. Instead of a birthday party with balloons and cake, the girls were dressed in white and sent to the Holy Chambers as the choir sang "Nearer My God to Thee." Once consecrated, the girls were expected to be available to the pastor at any time the Spirit called. One teenage girl ran away to a local farm. She was six months pregnant. The farmer contacted the county sheriff. A warrant was granted at once, and the raid was executed just as another consecration was underway. Matt caught news of the arrests via social media. He was in Alabama in a flash. His article published in *Mother Jones* was brutal. It suggested leaders of the community had to be aware. In fact, some were actual members of the congregation and participants themselves.

Matt's third project involved appalling conditions in an Arkansas chicken processing plant employing underage, undocumented migrants. It was published in *The Atlantic*. By then Matt decided to go freelance. He was asked to co-host a popular crime podcast, and this was a success as well.

Matt had just turned twenty-eight and was celebrating with Jeff Stout, his former professor from Yale. After several drinks and the usual banter, Jeff asked Matt "What are you working now?" Matt shifted uncomfortably and unclenched his hand to reach for his drink. Jeff could see Matt was clearly on edge. "You would not believe how difficult it is to find a good story. This year I chased three leads for months only to have them all fall through. It is competitive as hell. Seasoned investigative reporters are now offering money online for potential stories. I am beginning to wonder if my luck has run out."

Jeff responded, "Matt, cut it out. It was not luck that brought your success. You are a damn good journalist. That story in *Mother Jones* was dynamite." Jeff waited for his words to sink in before presenting an idea. "You know, Matt? I just might have the story for you. The Butlers of Bedford Landing, Kentucky." Matt rolled his eyes. The Butlers had been guests on several late-night shows in recent months and featured in all the home magazine articles. "No, seriously. Hear me out. My Aunt Ida Stout lives in Gayland, Kentucky, not far from Bedford Landing. She tells me there are tons of rumors about the Butlers and others in Bedford Landing ... how they got so rich so fast. Says it feels like a cult over there. Could be just small-town rivalry, but who knows?

The next morning Matt phoned Jeff Stout. "Hey! This is Matt. I've been researching. Guess who is going to spend a couple of weeks in Bedford Landing, Kentucky? Cannot pass up the chance to be there for what they are calling Butler Appreciation Day. You think your aunt would talk with me?"

When Matt called Ida Stout, she said, "Why, Mr. Conway, I am so pleased you are taking an interest in our small part of the world. Jeff told me to expect a call from you. He is so proud of his former students. Won't you come for tea at my house in Gayland? I may not have the details you need but would be happy to provide a few pointers." Before they concluded the call, Ida suggested "You must be sure to stay at the historic Bedford Landing Inn. It is a lovely place and many famous people have stayed there over the years. My very good friend Miss Anacelia Cline runs the Inn. We were sorority sisters together at Tulane, don't you know. Every year we have tea at the Waveland Mansion in Lexington. Please be sure to give her my regards."

# Bertha Roins Plans Her Move

Just a month before Bertha Roins arrived at the Bedford Landing Inn, she sat on an old sofa in a darkening room watching television. Bertha was a plump woman in her late sixties with a doughy face and thinning grey hair. Recently widowed and increasingly isolated, Bertha spent much of her time watching reruns of *Restore My Old House*. The phone rang. It was her nephew Paul Roins calling for the third time that day. This time she reluctantly answered. "Afternoon, Paul," she said flatly. "Good afternoon to you, Aunt Bertha. Don't want to be a bother, but I have not been able to reach you for over a week. Please tell me you're not planning to move to Bedford Landing." Bertha replied. "Paul, the matter is settled. I am renting this old house and buying a fixer upper in Bedford Landing." Paul quietly groaned. "Aunt Bertha, I am concerned you have not fully recovered from the shock of Uncle John's death and may regret this move." Her annoyance barely concealed, Bertha replied, "Paul, now don't you trouble yourself another minute. I am fine and need to get back to my program now. Goodbye." It was time for the Big Reveal on *Restore My Old House*.

Paul was her only living relative, albeit on John's side. She had never felt a familial connection but gladly accepted his help after John died. Paul helped her apply for survivor's benefits from the Ohio Police and Firefighter Fund, and he had been vigilant to ensure a prompt payout from John's life insurance as well. Still, she found Paul increasingly intrusive.

Bertha returned to the *Restore My Old House* rerun and silently recited the dialogue in unison with each character. On this episode, little Kaylene was helping her mother place cookbooks on the kitchen shelves as a finishing touch.

When the show ended, Bertha gazed fondly at a framed photograph resting on the end table next to her. The photo was of Clayton, Amy, and Kaylene Butler. She would proudly display the photo in her new home in Bedford Landing. There was a letter placed next to the photograph. After some time contemplating her future life in Bedford Landing, Bertha picked up the letter and re-read it in disdain. *The clerk who wrote this has no idea who I am. Clayton and Amy would never approve of this letter. I will make sure they know about this after I arrive in Bedford Landing.*

> *Dear Ms. Roins:*
> *We want to thank you for your most recent gift to our daughter Kaylene. As we have previously communicated to you, all gifts from fans are donated to the children's wing of the Bedford Landing Hospital. We kindly request you refrain from sending cards and gifts to our daughter. We know you will be happy to respect our privacy. This will be our last correspondence on the matter.*
>
> *Best Regards,*
> *Clayton and Amy Butler*

# The Death of John Roins

It had been six months since John Roins had fallen to his death at Sunset Cliffs in San Diego. Every year, tourists anxious for the perfect photo, risk their lives there. Like John, a number fall to their death.

Bertha and John had driven across country from Cincinnati to San Diego. John had hoped this trip would distract and dissuade Bertha from her newest obsession: moving to Bedford Landing, Kentucky. Throughout their marriage Bertha had chased dreams of the perfect life. Each time her plan was thwarted, Bertha struggled mightily with disappointment. Often violent outbursts followed.

As they pulled into a parking space at Sunset Cliffs National Park, Bertha began to badger John again. "John, I know this is the right thing for us. Why do you have to resist any new idea I have?" In exasperation, he replied, "Bertha, we have a perfectly good life in Cincinnati. Why can't you be happy with it? There is no one in Bedford Landing you know. What makes you think the Butlers would want anything to do with you? This is just another one of your fantasies and it has to stop now." Bertha jerked her chin and stepped out of the car. Looking back at him in barely concealed contempt, Bertha

# Death of John Roins at Sunset Cliffs

shouted, "Okay, John. Let's go get that picture before it turns dark. Wouldn't want *you* to be disappointed."

John had spoken for years about capturing this photo. He pictured himself standing at a cliff edge just as the sun sinks into the sea. Now a little unsteady on his feet after a recent stroke, Joe made his way to the perfect spot. Bertha called out, "Now just a minute, John. Let me adjust the focus. Move a little to the right. No, no, not that much. A little to the left. Yes, that is perfect. Now just take one step back. Take one more." As he did, both John and the sun vanished from view. Later in the dark, a small group watched the EMTs collect John's lifeless body from the jagged rocks below.

Bertha stood alone staring into the darkness. *With the payout from John's life insurance, I can have my house in Bedford Landing. And until I find it, I'll stay at Bedford Landing Inn. It has received such favorable reviews. Oh, the Butlers will be so pleased to see me.*

# Bertha Roins Explores Bedford Landing

On arrival at the Inn, Bertha was greeted by Miss Anacelia who gave her a guest welcome package. It included the Butler Restoration Trail map as well as brochures on the Story of Bedford Landing and Waveland Historic Site in nearby Lexington. Bertha smiled. "I am so happy to be in Bedford Landing at last. The pamphlet on Waveland Historic Site takes me back. My late husband John and I were never blessed with children. We always said how we regretted not having a little girl to take to the playground at Waveland Historic Site. You know I am moving to Bedford Landing and looking to buy a home. Would you happen to know a realtor?" Miss Anacelia answered. "I would be happy to provide a referral. After you get settled, please feel free to join our little social circle on the porch. Guests and some of our neighbors gather most evenings to discuss events of the day."

The next morning Bertha followed the Butler Restoration Trail map. To her delight, she was able to see all the homes renovated on *Restore My Old House*. At each house, Bertha stepped out of her car to reminisce about the episode. She was annoyed to encounter unwanted fans as she approached one house. The homeowner stormed out the front door and demanded the fans leave at once. Bertha was outraged. *These intruders were so annoying. Did they have no respect for privacy?*

That first week Bertha visited the Butler Farmhouse several times. From a distance, she could see their greenhouse and vegetable garden. Once she was thrilled to spot little Kaylene Butler chasing her dog. Kaylene was a petite five-year-old with blond, curly hair. It gave Bertha such pleasure to imagine how she and Kaylene would tend to the gardens on her Sunday afternoon visits. Kaylene would call her Nana.

However, Bertha sensed threat. More than once, she saw a red Mercedes 380 SL parked across the road from the Butler Farmhouse. A woman with dark hair and large sunglasses was watching Kaylene. Bertha found this intruder quite disturbing. *I will be certain to call this to the attention of Butler Security.*

It was paramount that Bertha find her house before Butler Appreciation Day. She met Cynthia Bolton downtown at Butler Realty. "Good afternoon, Ms. Bolton. I am Bertha Roins. Miss Anacelia Cline recommended you." "Why yes, Mrs. Roins. Miss Anacelia called me this morning and told me to expect you. Please take a seat. Would you care for something to drink?' Bertha smiled and declined. "Well then, Mrs. Roins. Please tell me what you have in mind?" Bertha answered without pause, "I would like to purchase a two bedroom/one bath bungalow close to downtown. There were several I saw on *Restore My Old House* I liked." Bertha was thrilled to learn there were three bungalows available, including the Kipping House. From watching reruns so many times Bertha was well acquainted with each. The Kipping House was the one favored by little Kaylene in Season 3 Episode 5.

Over the next few days, Bertha visited each bungalow and a few others as well. Although several would do nicely, she settled on the Kipping House. It had been built in 1955 by Gerald Kipping and occupied by the Kipping family until the year before. Bertha could just picture Kaylene sitting on the porch swing. On Friday after her arrival, Bertha extended an offer at $10,000 over the asking price.

That evening the porch regulars were all settled in their favorite chairs. Matt Conway and Bertha Roins joined them. After some light conversation, Miss Anacelia clinked her glass. "Ladies and gentlemen. I have a happy announcement. Mrs. Roins has made an offer on the Kipping house." Everyone congratulated Bertha, who beamed and patted her hair. Miss Anacelia made another round of cocktails.

Bertha's buoyant mood did not last. The very next morning, Cynthia Bolton called. "Mrs. Roins, I am afraid I have some bad news for you. Another buyer has made a cash offer on the Kipping house at $25,000 over the asking price." Bertha was livid. The Kipping House was meant for her and her alone. There was no doubt in her mind that the woman in the red Mercedes made the offer. It enraged her to think the woman would sit on that swing. "Mrs. Roins, I know you had your heart set on the Kipping house, but as I remember there were two others you liked as well. Would you consider visiting them again? I am available this afternoon." Taking a deep breath and repressing her fury, Bertha replied to Cynthia, "Well, dear, as my pastor in Cincinnati always says, 'Everything happens for a reason.' I will just have to choose from the other two." They made plans to meet at Butler Realty at 2:00 pm. The rest of the morning Bertha paced in her room pulling at her hair.

It was early Saturday afternoon. Miss Anacelia and Audrey sat next to each other on a burgundy Victorian settee in the parlor with

Cezanne squeezed in between them. They chatted quietly. Miss Anacelia was showing Audrey an old photo album of the Inn, pointing out notables who had been guests over the years. She was especially proud of the photo of A. B. "Happy" Chandler who always stayed at the Inn when campaigning for US Senator and Governor. "You know Happy Chandler served the Commonwealth of Kentucky for over 30 years. My mother said he always helped himself to a big breakfast."

"Oh, look. Here is a picture of the Great flood of 1937. I was told it was a cold January day when the Kentucky River busted from its banks. There was terrible damage to our town. And, oh my lord, Frankfort was a disaster!" A yellowish snapshot fell to the floor, and Audrey retrieved it. The picture was of four teenagers in swimsuits standing under Bedford Bridge. "Who is this, Miss Anacelia?" Before Miss Anacelia could respond, Audrey turned the photograph to see inscribed *Anacelia, Jeff, Lenwood and Lucas – Four Forever 1966*. Miss Anacelia gently took the photo from Audrey and fell silent. *There are only the two of us now.* Her grief never abated.

The quiet was broken by Audrey, "Mrs. Roins! You look upset. Are you okay?" Bertha stood before them and vacantly replied "I've lost the Kipping House." Audrey responded. "I am so sorry, Mrs. Roins. I know you had such high hopes for that house." Bertha replied. "Well, when you get to my age, you learn to move beyond life's disappointments, dear. This afternoon Cynthia Bolton and I are going to re-visit two houses." Audrey brightened. "Mrs. Roins would you like Miss Anacelia and me to join you? It would be fun. You can go, can't you Miss Anacelia?" Miss Anacelia nodded and smiled.

The visit to the two bungalows was not fun. In the afternoon light, the first house looked a little forlorn. The porch was small, and Bertha muttered something about a swing. They did not stay long. The Jubal

House on Oak Street was the better choice. It would require work, but that was expected. The payout from John Roins' life insurance would more than cover it. Still the Kipping House remained on Bertha's mind, and it rankled her to think how it was taken from her. She wandered through the rooms in the back and could be heard muttering about Kaylene's disappointment. Audrey and Miss Anacelia looked at each other in bewilderment. Then Cynthia called out to her, "Mrs. Roins, what do you think about this bungalow? It has a great porch, and you can easily add a swing." Returning to the living room, Bertha's response was abrupt and direct. "It will have to do. Go ahead today and make the same offer. I need to close on Monday or Tuesday to be ready for Butler Appreciation Day. Can you do that?" Cynthia was taken back by Bertha's tone and paused briefly before responding. "Why, yes, Mrs. Roins. The owner is in town. When I get back to the office, I will call him." Without another word, Bertha strode out the front door and down the steps to the car. Cynthia, Audrey, and Miss Anacelia were left standing speechless in the living room. On the return to the Inn, Bertha and Miss Anacelia were quiet. Audrey cheerfully chatted about her career aspirations in the entertainment business just to fill the awkward silence.

When the owner accepted her offer later that day, Bertha's sullenness lifted. *On Butler Appreciation Day, Clayton and Amy will ask me to join them on the bandstand. They will introduce me as the next homeowner to be featured on their show. I will be seen on television by everyone. Wonder what John would think now. He was always such a Doubting Thomas.* Her next step was to submit her application for *Restore My Old House*. She smiled, *A mere formality.*

# Sunday at Bedford Landing

It was a bright Sunday morning when Bertha arrived at the church where the Butlers worshipped. Services were about to begin. She wore a large pink silk carnation on her dress. When parking, Bertha spotted the red Mercedes that had been loitering at the Butler Farmhouse. With righteous determination, Bertha marched to that car. By then the majestic sound of the new pipe organ donated by the Butlers could be heard as Bertha deeply dug her key along the entire left side of the car. Entering the church, she took her seat in a back pew and joined the congregation in a superb soprano.

> *Praise God, from whom all blessings flow.*
> *Praise God, all creatures here below.*
> *Praise God above, ye heavenly host.*
> *Praise Father, Son, and Holy Ghost.*

Face beaming, Bertha always loved *Doxology*. Throughout the sermon, Bertha's eyes searched in vain for the Butlers. She was surprised to see that audacious Matt Conway seated toward the front. Bertha fumed. *The nerve of that young man. Just Friday, he had been snooping around at the diner and was asked to leave.* Her thoughts then returned to the Butlers, and she wondered if Kaylene was unwell. How happy she would have been to stay home with little Kaylene that morning. They would play Pretend Church with the stuffed toys. She imagined the entire service - hymns and all. For communion they would have grape juice and Kaylene's favorite cookies. Bertha moved her lips silently reciting imaginary conversations with Kaylene when her fantasy was interrupted by increasingly loud chatter all around her.

Services had ended, and the congregants were visiting with each other as they made their way down the aisle. Bertha was shocked to see how many bypassed the pastor and rushed through the door. *Clearly, they do not understand that church is a place where respect and reverence should be maintained.* It did not occur to her she had missed communion during her Pretend Church musings. Patting her hair, she waited in line until it was her turn. "Fine service, Reverend. My name is Mrs. Bertha Roins, and I am moving to Bedford Landing. Close friend of the Butlers, don't you know." The pastor's eyes gleamed at the prospect of another new congregant. "Why, we are always so happy to welcome another friend of the Butlers to our church family, Mrs. Roins." As she stepped on to the parking lot, she noticed the red Mercedes was gone.

It had become uncomfortably warm later that day. Miss Anacelia was feeling flushed and a little unsettled when she received a call from Paul Roins. "Good afternoon. My name is Paul Roins. I am nephew to Mrs. Bertha Roins. Can you please let me know if my Aunt Bertha is staying at your Inn?" Before Miss Anacelia could respond Paul went on to say, "You see, Aunt Bertha is not answering my calls and I do worry, given her nervous condition." Miss Anacelia was hesitant to become involved in the personal lives of her guests, but Paul persisted.

"If you could just ask her to return my call. There is urgent business that needs her attention." Miss Anacelia reluctantly agreed to relay Paul's request to Bertha and, an hour later she saw Bertha walking out to the porch with a large tote bag. "Afternoon, Bertha. I received a call from a young man claiming to be your nephew, Paul. Says he has been trying to reach you." Before Miss Anacelia could say more, Bertha cut her off. "Oh, Lord! Paul Roins again. Wish he would just leave me alone. Everything is perfectly fine." At that, Bertha left abruptly. Miss Anacelia studied one of the Pawpaw tree branches needing a trim when she felt a sudden chill. She whispered, "I just wonder if everything is perfectly fine."

That evening the porch regulars were discussing the upcoming Butler Appreciation Day festivities. No one knew exactly what to expect, but it seemed certain the fans would appear in droves in their RVs and campers. The Inn was fully booked for that weekend. Judge Northcutt excitedly announced, "We've had a last-minute change, don't you know. Now the Bedford Landing High School Band is to march around the square playing *Stars and Stripes Forever.* The committee can't decide whether to start the ceremony or end it with the march. What do you think, Miss Anacelia?"

Audrey was pondering how the marching band could make the biggest impact when she spotted flames shooting into the night sky. "Look over there, everybody. There's a fire!" she shouted. Judge Northcutt rose from his chair, leaned on the porch rail and craned his neck. "Well, I declare. That looks like the Kipping House. Ms. Roins, you have to be mighty relieved you did not buy that house." Bertha, who had just arrived on the porch, did not seem to hear him as she stared into the darkness. Audrey and Miss Anacelia briefly locked eyes and said nothing. Lucas was quiet as well. That night

## Susan DuVall

### The Kipping House Afire

the Kipping House burnt to the ground. Traces of Roman candles were found the next morning. The fire chief attributed the cause to youthful recklessness. He was reported to say, "Every year those dang firework stands pop up all over the county. Someone is gonna get killed one of these days."

# Matt Conway Investigation

The morning after Matt Conway arrived in Bedford Landing, he visited Jeff's aunt in nearby Gayland. Ida Stout was a spry lady in her eighties with an abounding curiosity. Her nephew Jeff often compared her to Agatha Christie's Miss Marple. She lived in an impeccably kept bungalow on a tree-lined street. Carefully tended flower beds graced her front yard. "Mr. Conway, so happy to have a friend and former student of Jeff's join us for tea. Jeff tells me you are a famous journalist." Two other ladies sitting primly on the sofa smiled politely. Matt replied, "Oh, you know Jeff. He is such an exaggerator. Still, ladies, I am grateful you have agreed to visit with me." "Do have some tea, Mr. Conway." "Call me Matt please." Ida beamed to have a celebrity in her home. "Cream and sugar, Matt?" Matt smiled, "Yes, ma'am." After another ten minutes exchanging pleasantries, Matt eased into the reason for his visit. "Ladies, as you know, I am an investigative reporter here to do a story on Bedford Landing and the Butlers in particular." Ida replied, "Well, they certainly have had a lot of favorable publicity this last year, and now I hear there are plans for a Butler Appreciation Day." Matt noticed all three ladies exchange disdainful looks. He let Ida's comments hang in the air for a while and then spoke gravely. "I am not here to write another laudatory article. On the contrary, my sources tell me there may be something of a cult operating in Bedford Landing." He waited for a response and got none. Finally, "Ladies is there anything you can share that might help me."

Ida Stout's replied solemnly. "Greed and fear make a perfect climate for cults, but if I were you, I would not overlook the wider question. How much of Bedford Landing is owned by outsiders now? Matt, I have read your articles and listened to your podcasts. You clearly have demonstrated familiarity with child labor laws, and I do not believe you are a complete stranger to our country's federal finance regulations."

When Matt pressed for details, he received none. Before leaving, Matt did learn that Ida Stout was not only a Master Gardener. She also served as Vice President at the Gayland Savings and Loan for twenty years.

Matt Conway's plan to interview the locals of Bedford Landing met with little success. News of his arrival spread quickly after the mayor's administrative assistant googled him. Matt's recent pieces in *Mother Jones* and *The Atlantic* were brutal. Mayor Alexander Louden was heard to say, "Matt Conway clearly has an agenda. We do not need to add fuel to his little project."

At lunchtime the next day, Matt took a seat at the Bedford Day Diner counter. After sipping his coffee for some time, Matt began a flirtation with the waitress Brenda Lee. She was in her twenties and the kind of girl easily overlooked. Leaning toward her he whispered in mock secrecy, "I wonder if you might care to have a drink with me tonight." Brenda Lee blushed and said, "Why we have not been formally introduced. My name is…" Just then the Bedford Day Diner manager appeared. "Brenda Lee, those customers in booth eight have been waiting for you to get their lunch." To Matt, he said, "Sir, we do not need to be formally introduced. I know who you are, and your business is not welcome here. I am asking you kindly to leave." As Matt stepped out the door, he could hear ugly mutterings among the customers. Bertha Roins seated in booth seven thought, *What a dreadful young man. He makes his living disparaging others. He is a vulture.* Brenda Lee sulked behind the counter feeling humiliated and cheated in life again. Ruefully she thought, *I never get to have any fun.*

The Bedford Day Diner was owned by the Butlers and the manager was cousin to Clayton Butler.

There was resistance from the clerk at the Bedford County Assessor office as well. Matt had researched online but wanted to see the property records related to secondary ownership of Butler Enterprises and some downtown businesses. "Well, Mr. Conway, we aren't here to do your research. Everything is online these days." Matt persisted, "I am asking to see the actual records." The clerk declined again prompting Matt to retort, "Are you aware of the Kentucky Open Records Act?" The clerk's face was pinched. "Yes sir. I am indeed. Now all you need to do is to file a Request to Inspect Public Records with the Office of the Secretary of State in Frankfort. You can find that form online as well. You from Kentucky, Mr. Conway? You need to be a resident of the Commonwealth of Kentucky." With that, the clerk returned to his paperwork and spoke no more.

The Bedford Landing Inn was Matt's best hope for a breakthrough. It did not take him long to recognize Lucas Todd and Audrey Willcox as resources. Neither was reluctant to speak with him.

Matt invited Audrey to dinner, and she shared her initial experiences as a Butler intern. "Maybe it is just that I am an outsider with too much imagination, but there is something weird about this entire operation. The employees have this eerie cult-like devotion to the Butlers not dissimilar to their wacko fans." Matt thought, *and not too dissimilar to the folks downtown*. Matt gently touched her hand. "Audrey, all my stories start from people with active imaginations. Anything you can bring would be helpful." Audrey was flattered and happy to find an ally close to her own age. She was lonely in Bedford Landing.

Lucas and Matt began staying on the porch after the others retired. Lucas shared how he watched Bedford Landing transform into a community increasingly foreign to him. "Matt, you are not the only one gettin' pushback. Old Jim Totten down at the *Bedford Courier* likes to say, 'It's like a damn iron curtain has dropped.'" Lucas continued, "Most city council meetings are closed now and business owners I've known for decades avoid my company. Then there are the migrant workers. I keep asking myself, *What in God's name are they doing with all those kids out there?*" Matt intended to find out.

Lucas Todd had lived in Bedford Landing his entire life except for his time in the military. He and his best friend Lenwood Yeager had joined the ROTC Kentucky Rangers. In Vietnam Lucas was shot in the leg. He returned home a more distant man. Lenwood did not return.

Events moved quickly after Lucas was accepted to law school in nearby Lexington. He met a girl working at the check-out counter at Winn Dixie. Not five months later she told him she was pregnant. They were duly wed, and Lucas faithfully endured a loveless marriage until his wife died five years before. Their only son lived in Seattle. Lucas rarely saw him.

One evening, Judge Hedger Northcutt remained behind on the porch with Lucas and Matt. Judge Northcutt hoped Matt might have pointers for the novel he and Lucas were writing. After all, Matt was an investigative reporter. "Well, gentlemen. I was fixin' to take my leave but would like to see what young Matthew has to say about eyedrop poisoning." Matt blanched at Judge Northcutt's words. "You see, Lucas and I have been pondering if it could go undetected. We understand just a few drops in someone's coffee could trigger a fatal heart attack. If the victim is elderly and has an existing heart ailment, I think it is unlikely an autopsy would be performed. Lucas has his doubts." Taking his lead from Miss Anacelia, Matt was slow to answer. "Judge, I find this a very clever proposition. There have been some reported convictions in recent years, but I am not certain of the actual circumstances of the crime. Seems to me this would require further research. I would be happy to collect whatever I can online." Satisfied his proposal for eyedrop poisoning would receive a fair hearing, Judge Hedger Northcutt retired for the evening leaving Matt and Lucas to their speculations about real-life intrigue at Bedford Landing.

Hedger was on the bench for twenty years and had earned a reputation for careful, if not protracted, deliberation. He now lived with his widowed sister Algean, who suffered from dementia. Her condition was worsening, and Hedger was unsure how much longer he could care for her. The mystery novel was his reprieve.

# Audrey Wilcox's Disturbing Day

The day after the Kipping House fire, Audrey made her way to work with the uneasy feeling she should never have accepted the internship with the Butlers. Something had felt "off" from the beginning. Her job was to support the Production Assistant for *Restore My Old House*. On the days when they were not shooting, Audrey worked Customer Service or ran errands. She dreaded the office. The women all wore white tops and navy skirts, reminding her of photos of flight attendants from another era. As an outsider, she was treated with thinly concealed contempt. No one ever made small talk with Audrey Wilcox.

That day, to her happy surprise, her assignment was to fetch wood shelves made in a neighboring county. The warehouse lead gave her keys to the company truck with directions to Weadock Wood and Ironworks. Audrey was wary of getting lost on the country roads and entered the destination in the GPS app on her phone.

It was another bright, sunny day. Off she went across Bedford Bridge and into the countryside. The route just happened to take her by the entrance to the Butler migrant camp where she spotted a number of *No Trespass* signs. Still Audrey was curious to take a quick look. Whenever the camp was mentioned at work, it was always done with a whisper. Pulling the truck over, she got out and peered down the old dirt road leading to the camp. It was lined on both sides by dense cornfields. The air was hot and humid and there was no wind. *This place is too spooky for me. I need to leave now,* decided Audrey.

What happened next caused her later to question her own senses and judgement. A small Latino boy was running down the old dirt road toward her. He was waving his arms and crying out "*Ayudame, ayudame, por favor!*" Audrey knew enough Spanish to understand the boy was pleading for help. She was mortified to see a large man suddenly appear from the cornfield. He grabbed the boy by the back of the neck with one hand and with the other slapped him across the face. The boy went limp. Audrey blinked and they were gone.

*This is a clear case of child abuse,* thought Audrey, but she was at a loss what action to take. She wondered if she should report the incident and to whom. *It all happened so fast. The camp was so foreboding with the* No Trespass *signs posted all over the place. Anyway, how do I know the man is not the boy's father?* Audrey got back in the truck and began to drive away. As she did, a black SUV with tinted windows tore out of the dirt road leaving a trail of dust. It was headed in the direction of Bedford Landing. Audrey glumly resumed her journey with the sinking feeling that she had betrayed the child.

Weadock Wood and Ironworks was in an old building near a junkyard of rusty cars. Tall weeds surrounded the building, much in need of paint. Davis Doyle Weadock was the sole proprietor as was his father before him. His work was featured on *Restore My Old House.* As the show gained in popularity, Weadock's revenue increased. He no longer had to bother with nuisance paperwork. The accountant at Butler Enterprises handled all his finances.

Weadock was a spindly man who was slightly bent from years leaning over worktables. His dingey, thin grey hair was pulled into a ponytail. When Audrey arrived, Weadock greeted her with a lascivious smile. "Good mornin', young lady. You must be Audrey from Butler. Here for the shelves?" Audrey nodded tentatively as Weadock coaxed her through the door, his bony fingers wrapped around her bare upper arm. "You look a little peaked, Audrey. Why don't you sit a spell while I load those shelves in the truck for you? As he walked to the back, Weadock turned to a small, furtive woman behind the counter and glowered. "Louise, get this girl a glass of water."

Louise handed Audrey the water. "Honey, did something happen to you on your way over here? You look real upset." Audrey turned her pale face to Louise and began to tell her about the boy at the migrant camp, the man who slapped him to the ground, and the strange SUV barreling out of the migrant camp. Louise listened intently, arms crossed as she pulled and pinched the skin behind her elbows. Audrey was not sure how long Weadock had been listening, but was startled when Weadock sharply interjected, "Miss, the shelves are in the truck. You best be on your way, and you drive real careful now. Wouldn't want you to get hurt." Again, that smile. Without looking at Louise, he uttered darkly, "Woman, don't you have something to do?" Louise wrapped her arms tightly around her thin waist and scurried to a dark room in the back. It was only then that Audrey noticed Louise had an ugly bruise on her arm. *What circle of Hell is this?*

Climbing into the cab of the truck, Audrey heard angry shouting. As she drove back to Bedford Landing, Audrey was haunted by the memory of the little boy and ashamed she did nothing to help him. He clearly was terrified and reached out to her for help. Then there was the way Louise cowered at Weadock's presence. Audrey wondered what happened to Louise after she left. It did not take Audrey long to begin to question what she thought she saw and heard. Had she lost perspective? This would not be the first time she misread a situation. There was that time when she thought a couple was kidnapping a little girl, and she called the police. It turned out the little girl was hearing impaired and did not know her parents were calling to her as she ran from them. Audrey cringed at the memory. *It was so embarrassing.*

Self-doubt took center stage in her thoughts. *That boy could well have skipped the camp school and was running to avoid punishment. Yes, the man did slap the little boy awfully hard, but is that egregious enough to notify authorities? Who would even be the authorities out here? Then there was Louise. She may not have been cowering at all. She could be just nosey and embarrassed that Weadock thought she was shirking her responsibilities. And what about Weadock? Is he a bully or just a rough kind of guy loyal to the Butlers like all the rest.* Then Audrey recalled the awful bruise Louise had on her arm. Suddenly, she was jarred out of her reverie when the truck began to swerve off the road. She set it right quickly and told herself. *It is time to quit conjecturing. Enough already.*

Crossing Bedford Bridge, Audrey felt immediate relief and looked forward to returning to the Inn after work. When she pulled up to the loading dock at the Butler warehouse, she saw a black SUV speed away. *You know? It looks exactly like… Don't even go there,* thought Audrey. She entered the building and could hear shouting. Knowing better, she did not announce herself. Instead, she crept deeper into the darkened warehouse where Amy and Clayton Butler stood not fifteen feet away. "Clayton, I want out and away from this. Look how those men talked down to you. Couldn't you see they were laughing at us? I just want to stick with the show and leave all of this other." Clayton scoffed, "You do not just walk away from people like this. Ask Haskell Crenshaw if you don't believe me." Bitterly Amy responded, "Yeah. Haskell Crenshaw. You were always so impressed by the Crenshaws. That is how you got us into this mess. Don't you know they think we are just poor white trash? You are now no better than a Crenshaw tenant farmer." Clayton's face turned purple with rage, and he slammed Amy against the shelving.

*I have got to get out of here now.* Turning quickly, Audrey bumped into a rack. Within seconds, Clayton appeared. He grabbed and twisted her arm. "What are you doing back here?" Audrey explained in a thin, tight voice that she was delivering shelves from Weadock Wood and Ironworks. Clayton took a long, hard look at her. "We don't take well to folks sneakin' around. You could get yourself hurt." Clayton released the grip on her arm and Audrey fled from the building. All she wanted was to get back to Miss Anacelia's Inn.

Returning to the Inn, Audrey hoped to see Miss Anacelia, but no one seemed to be around. *I think I just need to go to my room and regroup.* As Audrey began climbing the stairs and heard music. It was a recording of Van Morrison singing "Brown Eyed Girl." The music grew louder as she reached the top of the stairs. It was coming from Miss Anacelia's suite.

*Laughin' and a-runnin', hey, hey*
*Skippin' and a-jumpin'*
*In the misty mornin' fog with*
*Our, our hearts a-thumpin' and you*

Audrey peeked down the hall and was surprised to see Lucas Todd laughing and moving to the music at Miss Anacelia's door. Then a long slender arm reached through the doorway. *Oh, my God! Miss Anacelia just pulled Lucas Todd into her room. By his belt buckle!* Audrey quietly withdrew to her own room and fell into her bed. She did not want to think. Before falling into a deep sleep, Audrey heard laughing and

*Do you remember when we used to sing?*
*Sha-la-la, la-la, la-la, la-la, la-la, tee-da*

Audrey remained in her room until evening when she joined the group on the porch. She waited as the others retired and only Lucas and Matt remained. "Mr. Todd, can you all take a moment?" They could see she was clearly agitated. "There is something horribly wrong at Butler Enterprises, and after today I am not certain I belong there. I don't know what I should do. I really need this job for my resumé." Both Lucas and Matt leaned toward Audrey and gave their full attention as she recounted the events of the day. Miss Anacelia quietly sat on the settee in the parlor with Cezanne on her lap. The windows were open to catch the night breeze.

When Audrey finished her story, Matt began probing for more details. Lucas gently silenced Matt. "Whoa. Slow down, young man. Better you and Audrey talk tomorrow after she has rested." Then to Audrey, he firmly stated. "This is assault, pure and simple. Tomorrow, you should inform Sheriff Harlan Yeager. If you wish, I will accompany you to his office." Audrey's face registered anguish. "The last thing I need is to file a charge against my very first employer in the television industry. No one will ever want to hire me. Maybe I should just keep my head down and try to get through the Gibson house shoot. It is scheduled to be done in another week anyhow." Gently taking Audrey's hand, Lucas replied, "I understand your concerns and desire for a soft landing, my dear. Still, at a very minimum you should send me photos of that bruise on your arm tonight and again in the morning. I will document your account and serve as your attorney should need ever arise."

Matt excitedly offered to take the photos of Audrey's bruise. Lucas advised Matt to sit and not speak. By then, Audrey had regained her composure. "I will do as you suggest, Mr. Todd. Thank you so much for the guidance." Tracing the bruise on her arm, Audrey winced. Just then it occurred to her no one would suggest Louise out at Weadock Wood and Ironworks take a photo of her bruise.

From inside the parlor, Miss Anacelia grimaced at the thought of Clayton Butler ever touching Audrey again. *Not her guest. Not in her town.*

# Midnight Misadventure

It took little to convince Lucas to join Matt on a visit to the camp the next night. Both he and Miss Anacelia had become increasingly concerned about the children's well-being. For some reason, Sheriff Yaeger always deflected when he raised the subject. Lucas was puzzled. This was not like Harlan.

Crossing Bedford Bridge, they followed the same route Audrey took the previous day. At the dirt road entrance to the farm, Matt turned off the headlights and drove slowly down the bumpy road. At a distance, they saw lights. As they got closer, they heard the excited chatter of small children.

"Pull over here and keep quiet. No tellin' who we might run into." The car was parked precariously close to a ditch, and they struggled to get out of the car without making a noise. Moving closer, they could see a well-lit platform and the children encircling it. A short, heavy man mounted the platform and extended his arms forward with palms down. The children fell silent at once. Then a dark Cadillac appeared. Clayton and Amy Butler emerged and mounted the platform. The children stood at attention. When the short, heavy man opened his arms wide and lifted them to the sky, there was an explosion of cheers from the children. They screamed, "*Viva Butler, Viva Butler, Viva Butler.*"

Just then, Lucas felt the cold barrel of a shot gun shove deeply into his back. When he heard the hammer pulled back, he dropped his chin to his chest in dread. Matt was placed in a chokehold struggling to breathe. From the darkness came a disquietingly courteous voice. "Gentlemen, you really should be more cautious. A person could get hurt out here. Might never be found. Best you go on back home now." Matt was released and fell forward, coughing and gasping for air. Lucas felt the gun pulled from his back. The guards slipped into the darkness and Lucas whispered, "Matt, get your ass to the car now and don't look back." Matt raced to the car only to drop the keys in the dark, while Lucas struggled to hurry across the uneven ground. His leg injury from Vietnam had been troubling him of late. Once the keys were found and Lucas safely in the car, a flustered Matt pressed too hard on the accelerator and the car lurched forward straight into a ditch. When he tried to back up, the wheels began to spin. Finally, after several desperate maneuvers, the car was headed toward town with the exhaust pipe dragging. Viewing the entire scene with night vision binoculars was a man perched in a tree.

Neither spoke until they were on the porch. Miss Anacelia could see how rattled they were. Their clothes were rumpled, and Lucas' thick hair more disheveled than usual. She poured each a glass of bourbon and sat quietly with Cezanne in her lap. A few minutes passed when Matt suddenly blurted out, "They stood there like frickin' Juan and Eva Peron." Lucas could not help but smile. Miss Anacelia did not.

The next morning, Matt received a caller. Standing on the porch was a man in his forties wearing jogging clothes and a baseball cap.

"Mr. Conway, I need to have a private word with you. Would you join me for a walk? My name is Mason St. James, and I am with the FBI."

As they walked down the porch steps to the sidewalk, St. James turned to Matt. "Did you get enough excitement last night?" Matt continued walking and tried to appear at ease. St. James went on, "We are familiar with your reputation, Mr. Conway. But know this, you are stepping into very treacherous territory." Matt stopped walking and squarely faced St. James. "What the hell is going on out there?" St. James took a long look at Matt and responded. "All I can say to you, Mr. Conway, is back off. Do NOT go there again. You will be interfering with a federal investigation, and you could very well get yourself killed." In bewilderment, Matt watched St. James quickly turn and head toward downtown.

Matt was not the only person warned. That evening Lucas placed his hand firmly at Matt's elbow. "Son, no more midnight misadventures for now. You just need to let this thing percolate for a few days. You'll get your story."

# Bertha Roins Application

To appear on *Restore My Old House*, the candidate must already own the home. When making an application, hopefuls need to pitch their family story with photos and bio. The television audience would need to care about the homeowner. For her, Bertha knew this would all just be a formality. Still, she did not want to draw complaints of favoritism. Her plan was to follow the process and keep her special relationship with the Butlers to herself.

In her bio, she wrote it was in Bedford Landing she first met her husband, John. They both were on their way to Georgetown College, a small liberal arts college not far away. It was love at first sight and every five years on their anniversary they spent the weekend in Bedford Landing. Retiring in Bedford Landing was always their plan until John died in a tragic accident. Bertha wrote she planned to volunteer her days at the children's wing of the Bedford Landing hospital in John's honor.

John had never been to Bedford Landing. He loathed Bertha's obsession with *Restore My Old House*. The only true thing in the bio was that John was indeed dead.

The day had finally arrived for Bertha to submit her application to *Restore My Old House*. As she was dressing, Bertha imagined how it would feel walking into the office and announcing herself. She knew her entrance would likely not be filmed but she needed to be prepared. Already Bertha was beginning to feel her celebrity. Normally, she wore drab dresses with the same brown sweater. On this day she wore a flowery print dress and new high heel shoes.

Audrey and Miss Anacelia were the only ones at breakfast that day. They were seated in a Victorian dining room adorned with a stained-glass window, heavy flocked wallpaper, and an elaborate crystal chandelier. Audrey found the room magical and treasured this quiet time with Miss Anacelia. Miss Anacelia was sharing photos of her travels abroad and days as an equestrienne. For years, Miss Anacelia competed in jumping events at horse shows across the country. "I always preferred the elegance of Kentucky."

Miss Anacelia and Audrey looked up when they heard the loud clacking of Bertha's new heels on the wooden floor. There was a marked change in her appearance and demeanor. Normally sullen, Bertha exuded a manic energy. Seating herself with only coffee, Bertha began her chatter, "This morning I submit my application for *Restore My Old House*." Maybe it was the garish red lipstick or maybe the way she patted her hair. Whatever it was, Miss Anacelia and Audrey shifted uneasily in their chairs. Bertha exclaimed. "Oh, my goodness. Clayton, Amy, and little Kaylene will be so thrilled to finally have me appear on their show. I just cannot wait to hear what renovations they suggest. You know I have a few ideas myself for the breakfast room." Audrey and Miss Anacelia where surprised Bertha was acquainted with the Butlers, as she had never mentioned it before. *Or had she?* Neither wanted to ask and they smiled stiffly as she prattled on.

Later that morning, Bertha arrived at Butler Enterprises to present the application. She was filled with anticipation. Just as she imagined, the first thing she saw was a huge sign, reading: "Every child deserves to be cherished," located behind the reception desk. On the wall to her left, Bertha saw "before and after" photographs of all the homes renovated on *Restore My Old House*. She smiled as she knew every home so well. On the opposite wall, Bertha saw photographs of the Butler family posing with celebrities, including prominent Kentucky politicians and national television personalities. Bertha felt warm with pride.

A young receptionist in a navy skirt and crisp white blouse smiled brightly at Bertha. "Good afternoon, Ma'am. Lovely day, isn't it? How may we help you." Bertha proudly presented a large envelope to the receptionist. "I am here to submit my application for *Restore My Old House*." The receptionist glanced at the name on the envelope and paused before looking up with caution. In a flat voice she said, "Mrs. Roins, we will need to get back to you after a review of your application." Bertha was totally stunned and declared, "Don't you realize who I am? I am Mrs. Bertha Roins. Clayton and Amy Butler will want most certainly to see me." There was a fleeting grimace on the face of the receptionist. "Mr. and Mrs. Butler are not available. Again, Mrs. Roins, you will be contacted after your application is reviewed." With that, Bertha jerked her shoulder sharply. "I demand to speak to Ms. Audrey Wilcox." The receptionist struggled to maintain an impassive tone as she had been trained. "Ms. Wilcox is unavailable as well. Thank you for your application. Now you have a blessed day."

Bertha Roins name appeared on the "Fixated Persons" list at Butler Enterprises. She was not the only delusional fan obsessed with the Butler family.

Completely flummoxed, Bertha turned for the door muttering, "This receptionist has to be the same clerk who wrote that rude letter about sending gifts to Kaylene. I will see to it she is terminated forthwith." In a nearby hallway, Audrey stood aghast. Bertha saw Audrey's image reflected in the glass door as she left the building.

The visit from Bertha was reported to Security and a sense of hopelessness fell over Audrey after she was interviewed. Leaving work early again, she found Miss Anacelia sitting on the veranda in an oversized rocking chair with Cezanne in her lap. This was her private place and rarely visited by the porch regulars or guests. "Good afternoon, Audrey. Sit yourself down and tell me about your day." Audrey's eyes widened and she whispered. "Oh, Miss Anacelia. You will not believe what happened today when Mrs. Roins came to the office." Miss Anacelia leaned forward and said, "Do tell, Sweetie." Audrey took a chair near Miss Anacelia and shared the entire incident. "She seemed utterly unhinged, Miss Anacelia. It was so awful and so sad." Miss Anacelia felt no sympathy for Bertha Roins. What she felt was alarm.

Late that evening, Audrey returned to the veranda, looking out to the Kentucky River. It was a dark night, and the gazebo was barely visible. Everyone had long retired. She was thinking how it must have felt to watch the flood waters rising in the 1937 Great Flood. In a way, she felt she herself was watching flood waters rise. Leaning over the rail, Audrey felt a sharp blow to her lower back and tumbled over the rail. She was so stunned it took her a while to feel the sharp pain and understand what happened. Stumbling in the dark, she found the steps to the veranda. On the very top step, stood Cezanne watching her. She followed him through the darkened rooms and up the stairs. Cezanne scampered away as she reached her door. Once in her room with the door locked, Audrey sat on her bed and tried to collect herself. Then the ruminations started. *If I report this, would anyone believe me? After all, I did have two cocktails and smoked that joint with Matt. Is it possible I just lost my balance and imagined all of this? My back was bothering me earlier today.* The self-doubt was becoming overwhelming. Audrey turned to her phone's guided meditation app. The rushing thoughts began to dissipate. Soon she was asleep only to face another day in Bedford Landing.

# Bertha Roins Abysmal Rejection

It was the morning after Bertha submitted her application to appear on Restore My Old House. She was anxiously waiting for the acceptance letter when Miss Anacelia called her room. "Mrs. Roins, there is a gentleman here asking for you. He has some documents." Bertha was certain the Butlers had learned of the treatment she received and were mortified. They likely were sending an apology, perhaps even an invitation to dinner. Quickly smoothing her dress, she rushed down the stairs to see a small man in an ill-fitting suit. "Mrs. Bertha Roins?" Bertha nodded in anticipation. "I am here to deliver two documents. Would you please sign this form to acknowledge receipt?" Bertha officiously signed the form and was handed two envelopes. Without another word she returned to her room. Miss Anacelia saw the small man to the door. As he walked away, she wondered if Bertha had ever called her nephew Paul Roins.

**Letter One**

*Dear Ms. Roins:*
*After careful review, Butler Productions declines your application to appear on Restore This Old House. It is requested you make no*

*further applications. Please refer any questions you may have to Hoyle, Drayton, and Burks, Attorneys at Law. We wish you well in your future endeavors.*

*Martin Harricourt*
*Production Director*
*Bedford Landing, Kentucky*

**Letter Two**

*Dear Ms. Roins:*
*Enclosed is a restraining order issued by Judge John Heilman prohibiting you from further contact with Butler Productions, Clayton Butler, Amy Butler, and Kaylene Butler.*

*Randall Hoyle*
*Hoyle, Drayton, and Burks Attorneys at Law*
*Bedford Landing, Kentucky*

Bertha paced in her room throughout the day and late into the evening stopping only to catch her breath. The porch regulars had long departed when Bertha emerged. Standing at her door was Cezanne. Bertha placed her foot under his long, lean body, lifted him from the floor and rudely tossed him into the stair railing. Cezanne glared at her and scampered away. Bertha made her way down the stairs in a fog and wandered aimlessly through the dimly lit parlor, dining room, and into the office area set aside for guests. On the printer, she spotted a call sheet left by Audrey. It outlined where the cast and crew needed to be for the shoot in the morning. Kaylene was scheduled to appear on set at 11:15 am. Bertha tucked the call sheet under her arm and returned to her room.

# The Reckoning

Downtown Bedford Landing was a flurry of activity preparing for Butler Appreciation Day. The welcome banner was being draped across the front of the courthouse and American flags affixed to the bandstand. Storekeepers were placing Butler Appreciation posters on their walls and windows. Happily strolling the courthouse lawn was Mayor Alexander Louden who shook hands with anyone he met. Bedford Landing was sure to make a bundle the next day and he was certain to be re-elected in November.

While Bedford Landing was gaily preparing for Butler Appreciation Day, federal agents were executing search warrants at Butler Enterprises and Farm complex. Office employees were ordered out of the building. The ladies from Customer Service stood crying in the street as they watched FBI agents carry their computers and boxes from the building.

At the migrant camp, Lucas Todd and Matt Conway stood witness at a distance. Thin, terrified children were herded from the tents. Many wore no shoes. The smaller ones huddled together and began to whimper. From the surrounding fields, adult workers were rounded up

Migrant Workers at Butler Farm

as well. Their bodies were worn; their heads hung low. As they boarded the ICE buses, Matt, taking photos with his phone, remarked to Lucas, "They all looked so ashamed." Bitterly, Lucas answered, "No, Matt. They look like abused prisoners of war." After the buses left, Lucas and Matt observed agents removing evidence from the tents. They were carrying stacks of black denim jackets encrusted with turquoise.

Arrest warrants for Clayton and Amy Butler had been issued. Accompanied by their attorney, Randall Hoyle, the Butlers surrendered at the Sheriff's office where the task force had temporary headquarters. Agent Mason St. James was lead on the task force and was there to meet them. He was wearing a grey suit.

# *Kidnapping of Kaylene Butler*

It was 11:00 am when Kaylene and her nanny Mary Alison Todd arrived at the Gibson House. From outside everything looked normal. This was the final day of shooting before the Big Reveal, and Kaylene was to help her mother set the table. The fans always loved that scene. Kaylene, who was wearing a Butler signature jacket, popped out of the car and ran up the steps. She turned to wave before Mary Alison drove away.

What Kaylene found when she walked through the door was the Gibson House in chaos. After the search warrants were served that morning, filming was cancelled. No one thought to notify Kaylene's nanny. Clayton and Amy Butler had never made it to the set, and rumors were circulating wildly. The crew were rushing to put away the equipment. Many had already left, including Audrey Wilcox. Kaylene knew something was terribly wrong the minute she entered but did not know what to do. She began to cry, "I want my mommy." Just then a hand reached down and offered her a small teddy bear. It was Bertha who had gone unnoticed in all the confusion. She bent over with her face nearly touching Kaylene's. "Now don't you fret,

Kaylene. Everything is fine. Your mommy asked me to take you to a special playground for little girls." Bertha held Kaylene's hand a little too tightly. "Now you just come with me. We have cookies in the car." Kaylene was so confused. She had been taught to respect her elders and to mistrust strangers. She considered running but was too afraid of making Bertha angry. Once in the car, Bertha told Kaylene, "Now I am your Nana Bertha, and that is what you are to call me. Understand?" Kaylene nodded and tried to hold back her tears. It was about a 30-minute drive to Waveland State Historic Site. On the way, Bertha made Kaylene practice calling her Nana Bertha.

Mary Alison Todd ran errands after taking Kaylene to the Gibson House before stopping at the Bedford Day Diner for coffee. When she arrived, she was surprised to see every booth taken. At the back of the room, Butler employees were huddled around two booths. Everyone seemed to be talking at once in oddly hushed tones. Mary Alison bypassed the line and pushed her way to the Butler crowd. "Hey, what's going on?" The story of the raid began to unfold.

"The building was crawling with FBI."

"We were all forced out on the street. It was an outrage."

"They are taking away all the computers."

"Yeah, I heard they are out at Butler farm now. Clayton and Amy cannot be found anywhere."

"I heard they are in custody."

Mary Alison could not believe what she was hearing. Then she noticed crew members from the Gibson House. "So where is Kaylene?" she asked. "Isn't it your job to know," replied a rather contrary woman from Customer Service dressed in a navy skirt with crisp white shirt. The chatter resumed and Mary Alison realized she needed to act. She rushed back to the Gibson House to find it completely empty. Her hands trembling, Mary Alison called the Butler landline and mobile phones. No one picked up. A second later she called Lucas Todd.

Lucas was Mary Alison's uncle, and she always turned to him when there was trouble. "Uncle Lucas. Something terrible has happened. I've lost Kaylene." Lucas and Matt were driving back from the Butler migrant camp. After gathering as much information as he could from his distraught niece, Lucas calmly told her to remain in her car until he arrived at the Gibson House. He assured her they would find Kaylene, and everything would be fine. Lucas then called Sheriff Harlan Yeager and informed him the Butler child had gone missing. "God Almighty," shouted the Sheriff.

Lucas and Matt arrived at the Gibson House within minutes of Sheriff Yeager. Mary Alison was of little help, now sobbing in her car. The deputies were ordered to organize a search of the immediate perimeter and citizens of Bedford Landing were requested to aid. Volunteers poured into a hastily established command center in the same church basement renovated by the Butlers. A call for prayer was posted on the church Facebook page. Going unnoticed in all the excitement was Matt taking photos. It did not take long for them to initiate an Amber Alert.

# A Discovery in Bertha Roins Room

Audrey had returned to her room at the Inn wondering about her future. She called her mother Susan and was telling her about the raids when an Amber Alert sounded on her phone. "OMG, Mom. You won't believe this. I just got an Amber Alert. Someone has taken Kaylene Butler." Her mother responded "Well, Audrey, I always thought that whole setup was a tad sketchy, but you know your father…" "Mom, I gotta go now. Love you. Bye."

Audrey started down the hall to tell Miss Anacelia, when she saw Cezanne scampering out of Bertha's room with a pamphlet in his teeth. The door was slightly open, and Audrey called into the room, "Mrs. Roins, are you there? Mrs. Roins?" There was no answer. Just then Miss Anacelia appeared holding a chewed pamphlet for Waveland Historic Site. She gently pushed open the door. Bertha was not there. What they did find jarred Miss Anacelia and Audrey to their core.

The Victorian room was impeccably neat. On the desk was a framed family picture of Clayton, Amy, and Kaylene with a crudely cut photo of Bertha pasted next to Amy.

"Oh, my God. The woman is mad," whispered Miss Anacelia. Audrey rifled through the neatly stacked papers. "Here it is. The call sheet I lost. She had to have taken it from the printer last night. Kaylene's name is circled in red ink." Then Audrey saw the rejection letter from *Restore My Old House* and the restraining order. "Miss Anacelia. You really need to see this." Miss Anacelia glanced at the documents, reached into her apron pocket for her phone, and called Lucas Todd. "Lucas, you need to get over to the Inn now. Bring Harlan with you. I think we know who took Kaylene Butler."

It was only a matter of minutes before Sheriff Yeager and Lucas reached the Inn. They headed up to Bertha's room, taking two steps at a time. Matt followed as unobtrusively as he could. Upon entering the room, they found Audrey pointing into an open closet. "You will find Roman Candles in that bag," she announced. Miss Anacelia beckoned Lucas and Harlan to the desk to see the framed photo of the Butlers and Bertha Roins. She handed both documents to Sheriff Yeager. "Harlan, the Butlers took out a restraining order on Bertha Roins." Sheriff Yeager was on his phone at once. Then two sheriff deputies appeared. The small room was getting crowded. Audrey tried to explain to anyone who would listen the significance of the call sheet.

The pamphlet was still in Miss Anacelia's hand when she recalled Bertha's words, *"My late husband John Roins and I were never blessed with children. We always said how we regretted not having a little girl to take to the playground at Waveland Historic Site."* Miss Anacelia handed the pamphlet to Lucas. "I think I know where Bertha has taken Kaylene. We need to get there now. There is no tellin' what she might do. You can see she is clearly demented." Just then one of the deputies pulled Lucas away to answer a question related to evidence handling. The Sheriff was still on the phone discussing the restraining order. Matt was photographing the bag of Roman Candles.

Miss Anacelia interrupted Lucas and the deputies. "This cannot wait." Before Lucas could say, "Now just a minute, Miss Anacelia," Lucas became distracted by Sheriff Yeager who wanted to share what he learned about the restraining order. When Lucas turned around, Audrey and Miss Anacelia were gone. Looking for them out the window, Lucas only saw a purple sky and gathering storm. It was a perfect photo for Matt.

# Rescue at Waveland State Historic Site

The storm was approaching as they drove to Waveland Historic Site. Miss Anacelia said ruefully, "I knew from the beginning that woman was not right. It was clear she was obsessed with little Kaylene Butler. How I regret not calling Amy." Audrey replied, "Miss Anacelia. You cannot blame yourself for this. The Butlers knew she was in town. Remember they had her on a "Fixated Persons" list and issued the restraining order. There was nothing you could have done." After a pause Audrey ventured, "There is this thing that happened Wednesday night I never mentioned. It was late, and I was leaning on the veranda rail thinking about the Flood of 1937. It felt as if someone poked me hard in my lower back. I lost my balance and fell over the rail." Miss Anacelia gasped, "Audrey, you should have told us. Why didn't you tell us?" "Well, I was embarrassed. It was so dark, and I had been drinking. What if no one believed me? Then I started to wonder if it was my imagination, but you know what? I think it was Bertha Roins. That was the day she behaved so erratically at the office. I am sure she saw me on her way out the door. Does that sound crazy? Miss Anacelia answered sharply "Audrey, I do not believe the fall was an accident at all. Bertha Roins is not only deranged. She is vindictive. Lucas thought something was wrong from the beginning. Recall how bitter she was about the Kipping house? And why on God's green earth would a woman her age have Roman Candles in her room? She is dangerous, Audrey." "Miss Anacelia, what might she do to little Kaylene?" Miss Anacelia did not answer but accelerated the car, her hands tight on the wheel.

The storm was approaching when Miss Anacelia and Audrey arrived at Waveland. The last tour group of the day was assembled near the mansion, and their guide was hurriedly completing her talk. Audrey and Miss Anacelia approached them from behind. They could see Bertha with Kaylene still wearing her Butler signature jacket. Audrey's heart was pounding. She rushed the group and pulled Kaylene away from Bertha. Everyone in the tour group turned in shock to face Audrey. *Oh my God*, Audrey was mortified. The little girl was not Kaylene, and the woman was not Bertha. "Whatever do you think you are doing?" shouted the tour guide. Audrey felt her knees slightly buckle. She apologized profusely and turned to Miss Anacelia who stood scanning the landscape. At a distance, she spotted a woman with a little girl who also wore a Butler signature jacket. They quietly made their way down the hill to the playground. It was not long before law enforcement led by Sheriff Harlan Yeager arrived at Waveland only to make the same misidentification. The tour guide was appalled. As the officers backed away in complete embarrassment, the tour guide silently raised her arm and pointed down the hill.

The sky was darkening now as Audrey and Miss Anacelia arrived at the playground. Bertha was erratically pushing Kaylene in the swing singing in a perfect soprano,

*Over the river and through the woods to grandmother's house we go*
*The horse knows the way to carry the sleigh,*
*Through the white and drifted snow.*

There was a crack of thunder and lightning shot across the sky. That is when Bertha noticed Audrey and Miss Anacelia. Bertha's expressionless face quickly contorted, and she began to push Kaylene harder and sang louder. By then law enforcement had arrived to see Kaylene dangling from the swing seat, her face drawn in terror.

What happened next will live in the memory of Bedford Landing for years to come. Pointing her finger at Bertha, Miss Anacelia roared so loudly it could be heard across the estate. For a split second everyone froze in bewilderment. Those who were present recalled later that Kaylene seemed suspended in the air. Then in answer to Miss Anacelia's exhortation, Audrey charged Bertha taking her down hard.

Just as quickly a law enforcement officer sprang from his position and grabbed Kaylene from the crazily spinning swing. Bertha was cuffed and taken away. It was all over in 90 seconds. The rain was now coming down in torrents, and who should appear but Lucas Todd offering Miss Anacelia his umbrella. She had begun to shiver. Sheriff Yeager approached them and made a slight bow. "Honor to know you, Miss Anacelia. You all can go on back to Bedford Landing now. We'll take statements in the morning." Miss Anacelia took his hand in both of hers and gently nodded. Since the death of their close friend Lenwood Yeager in Vietnam, Miss Anacelia and Lucas Todd watched over his younger brother Harlan, taking pride in all he accomplished and encouraging when he needed.

Matt Conway had arrived at Waveland with Lucas. He was frantically taking photographs when he noticed Lucas, Miss Anacelia,

# Susan DuVall

*Kidnapped Kaylene*

and Audrey walking hurriedly toward the car. Racing to catch up, he stumbled into Audrey. "Hey," said Audrey indignantly. "Hey yourself, Audrey. How is it every time I turn around you are in the middle of my story?" Audrey smiled and replied. "It isn't just your story, Matt."

That evening Miss Anacelia invited Lucas, Matt, and Audrey for dinner. Her cook and inn manager was Landry Gelpi of New Orleans. Using produce from the Inn's herb and vegetable garden, Gelpi served his specialty and Inn favorite: Jambalaya, fried green tomatoes, and sweet potato pie. Somehow Judge Hedger Northcutt managed to show up just in time to join them. He had been laboring all day on the novel. Secluded in his study, he was oblivious to the events of the day.

When they were all seated at the table, Judge Northcutt said "You know, Lucas? What would you think about this development? At the end of Chapter 8 the body of the pastor is found hanging from a rafter in the tobacco barn?" Miss Anacelia gently replied. "Hedger, this is a very intriguing twist that will require considerable deliberation. Tonight, why don't we just enjoy this fine meal Mr. Gelpi has prepared?" Judge Northcutt looked a little befuddled. "Why, of course, Miss Anacelia." As they dined in silence, the rain pounded against the metal roof of the Inn. After dinner, everyone quietly retired. There was no porch talk that evening.

# Butler Appreciation Day

Butler Appreciation Day brought brilliant blue skies after the terrible storm the night before. Around 8:00 that morning a trickle of RVs and campers began to stream into town. They were greeted by strangely empty streets and sidewalks. The bandstand stood forlornly on the courthouse lawn and the welcome banner had fallen to the ground.

Stunned business leaders and city council members were secluded in their homes. Mayor Louden glumly sat in the office of his attorney preparing for an interview with federal investigators. If he made a wrong move, his political aspirations would be in jeopardy. Shops normally open at 9:00 am on Saturdays would remain closed that day and bewildered fans wandered aimlessly on the courthouse lawn. That day Bedford Landing was a well-maintained ghost town.

In the evening, there was a solemn gathering on the porch of the Bedford Landing Inn. Guests and porch regulars nursed their bourbon and spoke little. Everyone was anxious for details. Throughout the day Lucas Todd had been in contact with the Sheriff Harlan Yaeger. He and Matt were permitted to speak briefly with Special Investigator Mason St. James as well.

Finally, Lucas leaned back in his chair and began to share what they learned. "Nearly a year ago, there was an anonymous call on the federal Trafficking Tip Line about Butler Enterprises." Audrey shifted in her chair so excited to be part of the drama. Lucas continued. "It led to the formation of a joint task force from the US Treasury, Homeland Security, and the FBI. Naturally, Sheriff Yeager was the local law enforcement liaison." Miss Anacelia nodded with pride. "After extensive, clandestine monitoring, the investigation found probable cause to believe Butler Enterprises and others in Bedford County were engaged in money laundering, wire fraud, and forced labor." Audrey recalled her mother's last words to her, "*Well, Audrey, I always thought that whole setup was a tad sketchy…*"

Lucas continued, "It is believed that Haskell Crenshaw initiated the *entire* enterprise. He is heavily in debt and has contacts with one of the Mexican cartels. Clayton Butler allowed himself to be used by Haskell Crenshaw and poor Amy went along."

Judge Northcutt remarked, "I heard Haskell had run his business into the ground and his uncles were losing patience. And you know, I always wondered how the Butlers were able to diversify so quickly. Neither had any business experience. Before their TV show, he did odd jobs and she worked at the paint store."

Matt could not contain himself. "I wondered the same thing myself and spoke with Jim Totten at the *Bedford Courier* today. He thinks the Butlers, coming from humble circumstances, were in awe of the Crenshaw family. It was easy for Haskell Crenshaw to manipulate them. Crenshaw provided the accountant and financial advisors. Clayton Butler went along with whatever they said. Others in Bedford County were enlisted as well, taken in by the celebrity associated with *Restore My Old House*. To quote Jim Totten, "When prosperity, fear, and secrecy are linked there is a perfect breeding ground for malfeasance."

It came as no surprise to Miss Anacelia that the Crenshaws were involved. They were known for unsavory business practices as well as exploiting vulnerable locals. Miss Anacelia only prayed that her friend Cynthia Bolton had not been used by them. Audrey's thoughts went to Weadock Wood and Ironworks. *Of course, that slimeball was involved!*

Judge Northcutt asked. "What about the farm workers and those kids?" "Well, I can tell you this much." answered Lucas. "They ran that farm like a cult. The workers were half-starved and isolated from the outside world. All their papers taken from them, and the children, many undocumented, were kept in separate tents where they worked day and night on those denim jackets." Matt interjected, "Lucas and I saw with our own eyes." He started to recount their misadventure at the farm when Lucas gently shushed him.

Lucas continued, "The migrant children and adults have been taken to separate ICE facilities. It is clear both adults and children were abused and underfed. I understand a team of medical professionals are assessing their health and the health risk to the community. Homeland Security has engaged the Mexican, Honduran, and Guatemalan governments to assist in the return of the workers to their home countries. The disposition of the unaccompanied minors will be an entirely different challenge. They may never find their way home." Under his breath Matt uttered the motto of Amy Butler: *Every child deserves to be cherished.*

Lucas paused for a minute and then concluded his narration, "The damage to our town's reputation is incalculable." Judge Northcutt would now grieve for the community he loved as well as the sister drifting away from Alzheimer's.

To no one's surprise the network cancelled *Restore My Old House*. There would be no more reruns for Bertha Roins to watch. Nearly everyone employed at Butler Enterprises was let go, including Audrey Wilcox. The company was now a skeletal operation with only one function, providing subpoenaed information to the federal task force. The former employees were devastated.

When discussion of Butler Enterprises slowed, Judge Northcutt asked, "Miss Anacelia, do you know what became of Mrs. Roins?" Before sharing, Miss Anacelia refreshed everyone's drinks. Audrey thought to herself. *We did not drink this much in college.* Miss Anacelia sat up straight with Cezanne at her side and began. "Well, after Bertha was seized at Waveland, she was taken to UK Eastern State Hospital. Now please understand what I will tell you next is confidential." Miss Anacelia paused, and Audrey could barely stay still in her seat. "Bertha underwent an evaluation by a state psychiatrist. She insisted it was all a terrible mistake by law enforcement…that she was a friend of the Butlers who considered her a 'Nana' to little Kaylene Butler. When the psychiatrist seemed to doubt her, Bertha lunged across the table and pummeled him. It took two guards to pull her off. Bertha remains at the hospital heavily medicated."

"There is a relative, don't you know. Later today I was able to reach Paul Roins, Bertha's nephew. He had called on Sunday, inquiring about her. Bertha had not responded to his calls. When I summarized the events, Paul did not seem at all shocked. He told me this was not the first time his Aunt Bertha had been institutionalized!" Unable to contain himself, Matt leaned to Miss Anacelia. "Can you give me Paul Roins contact info?" Everyone on the porch looked at him in exasperation. Lucas smiled. "Not the time, Matt."

After Miss Anacelia had completed her account, Judge Northcutt stood to attention and invited everyone to raise a glass to Miss Anacelia and Audrey for their valor in taking down Bertha Roins. Everyone stood as Miss Anacelia quietly petted Cezanne and Audrey beamed.

Then Judge Northcutt asked Audrey what her plans were now that she was unemployed. Audrey wrinkled her nose and slightly tilted her head. "You know, I am not entirely certain a career in film and television is my future. I have been thinking about going back to school. Special Investigator Mason St. James suggests I consider applying to John Jay College of Justice in New York City. He says they have a great Psychology and Crime program." Matt blurted out, "So how do you know Mason St. James?" "Oh," said Audrey, "We met at the Bedford Landing Library a couple of times. I helped him with the investigation. Never would have considered it as a career in forensic psychology until I came to Bedford Landing." Just then Audrey saw a shiny red Mercedes pass by the house. It was not the first time she had seen that car.

## *The End*

# Part Two
# The Crown Jewel

# Contents

| | |
|---|---|
| Recovery and Return | 91 |
| Pawpaw Salsa | 95 |
| Honor and Recognition | 101 |
| Bedford County Tobacco Festival | 107 |
| Undaunted | 111 |
| Crenshaw Grievance | 117 |
| Community Spirit | 121 |
| Fixation | 125 |
| A Curious Visitor | 127 |
| Secure the Locks | 131 |
| Decorum | 133 |
| Bombshell at the Bistro | 137 |
| Grooming | 141 |
| Anticipation and Dread | 145 |
| Betrayal | 149 |
| Lest We Ever Forget | 153 |
| Discovery | 157 |
| Media Sensation | 161 |

# Recovery and Return

The Butler family and their highly successful home decoration show *Restore My Old House* was the pride of Bedford Landing. Mayor Alexander Louden often boasted that Bedford Landing now ranked as #7 in the top ten destination spots for renovation enthusiasts. He enjoyed pulling a magazine clipping from his pocket to validate this claim.

All that changed when a joint federal task force conducted a raid of Butler Enterprises and farm. What they found on the farm appalled the community. Then the unthinkable occurred. A deranged, delusionary super-fan kidnapped little Kaylene Butler that very same day!

When the story broke, Bedford Landing gained national attention and became known in the tabloids as the "Cult on the Kentucky River." The network quietly cancelled the show and discontinued all reruns. It was reported that a federal grand jury would be convened to investigate human trafficking, forced labor, and money laundering. No longer were the Butlers the "Pride of Bedford Landing." They had brought disgrace and shame to the town.

As the summer passed, national interest in the story waned and the town's spirit began to revive. Afterall, the Bedford County Tobacco

Festival was coming up the first of October. The planning co-chairs were Judge Hedger Northcutt and the mayor's wife, Grace Louden, who were determined for success. The first Tobacco Festival was held in 1948 as the country was recovering from a world war and veterans struggled to return to their lives. Bedford Landing was now undergoing its own recovery and return.

Enter Miss Anacelia Cline's nephew from New Orleans. Joe Cline had an irrepressible zeal to transform Bedford Landing into a cultural center. It would be modelled after Berea, Kentucky, known for its art festivals, historic district, and fine restaurants. Business rescue and reimage were not new to Joe. He became a very wealthy man doing just that after Hurricane Katrina. To this day folks in Bedford Landing argue. Was Joe Cline an opportunist or a visionary?

What could not be disputed was this. An attempt of mass murder was visited upon the town of Bedford Landing after Joe Cline's fervor ignited both ancient rivalries and a continued, obsessive quest for celebrity among certain town residents.

# Pawpaw Salsa at The Inn

It was a cool September night, and an early fall was expected. Soon the chestnut trees at Bedford Landing Inn would show their brilliant yellow leaves to the delight of the town. The pawpaw trees had begun to give up their fruit for pudding and shortbread. This year Bedford Landing Inn's chef and manager Landry Gelpi experimented with pawpaw salsa to great success, settling on what would soon become a famous recipe:

**Landry Gelpi Pawpaw Salsa**
- ½ cup ripe pawpaw flesh (deseeded and cubed)
- 1/3 cup diced red onion
- 1/2 diced medium green bell pepper
- 1 ½ cup Roma tomatoes (seeds removed and cubed)
- 2 tablespoons lime juice
- 1/2 teaspoon Creole seasoning
- 1 ½ tables spoon fresh minced cilantro
- 1/2 minced jalapeno pepper

Mix together and chill for 2 hours before serving.

Miss Anacelia's nephew Joe Cline and his partner Peter Honoré joined the others on the porch that evening. They made their home in New Orleans but had become regular weekend visitors since the raid and kidnapping story broke.

One evening in early July, Joe and Peter were stunned to see Miss Anacelia's face appear on CNN with the caption *Innkeeper Thwarts Kidnapping while FBI Raids Kentucky Town*. Within minutes, Joe called Miss Anacelia.

"Auntie A! Are you okay? What on earth is happening up there in Bedford Landing?"

At age twelve, Joe had been left in the care of his aunt after the death of his parents. He felt as protective of her as she him. There were some difficult years for Joe after his parents' fatal car crash, but ultimately, he rallied. Following Miss Anacelia's lead, Joe attended Tulane University and chose to make New Orleans his home. Throughout the years, Miss Anacelia and Joe remained close as he built his considerable wealth as an investor. They often visited one another. On the tenth anniversary of Katrina, Miss Anacelia proudly watched as Joe was honored by the New Orleans Betterment Society for his tireless effort promoting public art in the city.

At 35, Joe was mindful of his appearance. He worked out nearly every day and rode his bike with Peter through the streets of New Orleans on weekends. More than once, Miss Anacelia was taken by the similarity in appearance and bearing Joe shared with his father and her brother, Dr. Jefferson Cline. Both were tall and lean with sandy hair. Each had boundless energy and could quickly gain the confidence of others with their easy way of speaking. Jefferson used these gifts to benefit his less affluent patients whereas Joe's used the gifts to build wealth and public profile.

On his first visit to Bedford Landing after the raid, it was clear the Butlers would be unable to hang on to the Bedford Day Diner or the Mercantile given their crushing legal fees. Joe offered to relieve them of the burden. The diner was to be transformed into the Bedford Bistro and the Mercantile to the Bedford Art Consortium. Joe had lofty plans for Bedford Landing and was confident other investors would follow.

At 28, Joe's partner Peter Honoré was less aspirational. He was a small, quick man of Creole descent who had strong family roots in Louisiana. He and Joe attended Peter's frequent family celebrations. The food was always "spectacular" according to Joe. Peter had worked as a chef in New Orleans for 10 years. His last job ended in a dispute involving scallions, and he had been searching for a new opportunity ever since. Now he was standing up the Bedford Bistro. The menu would offer Creole and Kentucky fare in which pawpaw salsa was a requirement. Joe and Peter planned to operate their businesses from New Orleans, while Landry Gelpi would provide local management oversight.

As Miss Anacelia was serving cocktails to her porch guests, the conversation turned from weather to Clayton Butler. Judge Hedger Northcutt declared. "Seems Clayton Butler made a spectacle of himself again this afternoon. He was on the courthouse lawn drunk as Cooter Brown hollering something about the Crenshaws." Lucas Todd gravely added, "The situation is worsening by the day. I've been told Amy Butler showed up at the hospital with a broken collar bone and black eye two days ago." Miss Anacelia took her seat with her long-haired dachshund Cezanne and spoke. "Gentlemen, you may not be aware, but the Bedford Landing Ladies Auxiliary has stepped in to help Amy Butler. Clayton has moved out of the Butler Farmhouse now and Amy is looking to find her own attorney. We hoped you might help us with that, Lucas." Lucas replied, "It would be my pleasure to be of assistance to Mrs. Butler."

Peter leaned into Joe and asked, "Who's Cooter Brown?" Lucas Todd was seated next to Miss Anacelia intoned in his deep voice, "Legend has it, Peter, there was once a gentleman named Cooter Brown. Mr. Brown chose to stay intoxicated on the Mason-Dixon line during the entire War Between the States. In that way, he avoided the draft on either side, don't you see."

When the laughter subsided, Judge Northcutt paused rocking his chair and leaned toward Joe, "Mr. Cline, word has it you will be open for business by Tobacco Festival time. You know I am the co-chairman of the festival this year." Joe was quick to respond. "Judge, you can count on it. Fully operational in two weeks. Bedford Landing is on its way to become a Kentucky cultural jewel."

Miss Anacelia shifted uneasily in her seat. She was proud of her nephew Joe but was concerned his occasional bombast could invite trouble. *I do wish Joe would tone it down a bit.* She could not but wonder if Joe's motivation to renew Bedford Landing was in large part to rankle Haskell Crenshaw. Haskell was Joe's childhood tormentor years ago and the wounds had never healed.

Conversation had turned to the upcoming grand jury when Haskell Crenshaw himself appeared out of the darkness on the porch steps. He was a tall, rangy man with thinning red hair. Haskell often spoke proudly of his days playing basketball at Georgetown College and remained fit for many years. Then over time alcohol and prescription drug abuse drove his declining health, erratic behavior, and devastating business losses. Most folks in town avoided him.

"Good evening, you all. Enjoying this fine September night? Miss Anacelia, I must say your chestnut and pawpaw trees are always the talk of the neighborhood." She made no response and Haskell turned his attention to Joe. "Why, Mr. Cline, you and your boyfriend here seem to be making quite a name for yourselves in Bedford Landing. Folks been calling you all *Vulture Enterprises,* or did I hear *Bottom Feeders Ltd*?" Haskell shot a menacing smile at the group on the porch showing his bad teeth and emitted a high pitch laugh. "I dunno… I forget." Then to Joe, "Anyhow I know you must just be thrilled to have the opportunity to spend time with your aunt here." And with a slight bow, "Miss Anacelia, I sure hope you are takin' good care of that cute little dog. It would be a shame for anything to ever happen to him." Cezanne leapt from Miss Anacelia's lap and glared at Haskell in disdain.

Hands resting quietly in her lap, Miss Anacelia leaned toward Haskell and spoke, "Why, Haskell, you need to take care as well. Not sure but you may have had a bit too much to drink tonight. Probably best you run along home now. I am sure your wife wonders where you are." Totally discombobulated, Haskell wandered into the night. His wife Ruth Anne left him a year before and took the children.

Joe stood by Miss Anacelia and said not a word. The others on the porch remained silent until Lucas Todd darkly pronounced, "That boy will come to a bad end. Always was trouble."

## Susan DuVall

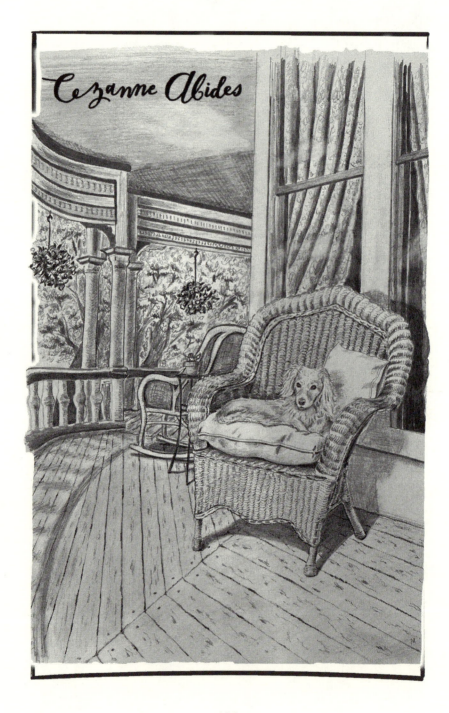

# *Honor and Recognition*

Miss Anacelia and Landry Gelpi were seated at the kitchen table planning the menu for the upcoming week when Judge Hedger Northcutt burst through the door knocking Gelpi's prize copper utensils off the wall. Northcutt's face was flushed, and he was breathing heavily. "I will NEVER work with that woman again. We are just weeks away from the festival, and the parade marching order still isn't finalized." Gelpi carefully retrieved each utensil from the floor and Miss Anacelia guided the Judge to a chair. "Hedger, now why don't you sit right here and quiet yourself. Landry will get you a cup of coffee."

Miss Anacelia was fully aware of the conundrum. The Future Farmers of America and the 4-H were engaged in fierce competition over who would lead the parade. Both clubs were actively campaigning for the honor. Each blamed the other for the previous year's debacle when an ugly incident occurred just as the parade ended. Boys from both clubs began shooting at each other with high powered water guns. Initially, the crowd was amused at their antics, but then the boys began aiming indiscriminately. Some onlookers were drenched. No one ever knew who brought the paintball gun, but no one there could ever forget the Tobacco Festival Queen seated on her float weeping. Her lovely yellow dress was covered with black paint splatter and her long curls ruined. The next day Jim Totten wrote a scathing editorial in the *Bedford Courier* condemning the brawl. It did not take long for the finger pointing to begin and loyalty lines to be drawn.

Grace Louden had waffled for weeks trying to avoid alienating voters on either side. Her husband, the mayor, was campaigning for re-election and still struggling with the Butler stigma. Miss Anacelia waited until the Judge had calmed himself before offering a suggestion. "Well, you know, Hedger. I have been giving some thought to the issue. Perhaps you and Mrs. Louden can join me for tea. I wonder if we just might find a compromise."

The following afternoon, Miss Anacelia dressed in a long periwinkle skirt and white linen top greeted Grace Louden with a welcoming smile. "Good afternoon, Grace. I am so happy you could join Hedger and me for tea." The Judge had already arrived and sat anxiously in the parlor. He was wearing his best blue seersucker suit. "It is so lovely outside." Miss Anacelia said "Won't you all join me on the veranda? Mr. Gelpi has prepared a table for us."

Grace Louden was a slim woman in her forties with long blond hair. That afternoon she wore a red knock-off designer suit with three-inch heels. With campaigning in mind, Grace was aware of the importance of her public image and had adopted the style of television newscasters. This meant eyelash and hair extensions as well as regular Botox treatments. When her husband complained about the cost, she would remind him this was a necessary expense given their political aspirations. Grace expected someday to be First Lady of the Commonwealth of Kentucky.

After they assumed their seats on the veranda, Grace gazed onto the Inn grounds. "Miss Anacelia, your gazebo is so lovely. I did not realize you had such a fine view of the river." Pouring a cup of tea for Grace, Miss Anacelia replied, "I have such fond memories playing out there as a child." The conversation drifted a few minutes when Miss Anacelia said, "Grace, I know you and Hedger want to reach the right decision for the parade and how mindful you are of the strong sentiments on both sides. It just occurs to me we need to relegate last year's dreadful incident to the past. You know, I am not entirely certain it was a Bedford County boy who sprayed the black paint. More than once, I heard it suggested the ruffian was from Maddox County. You recall he was said to be wearing large goggles."

Grace pounced. "Miss Anacelia, I have to agree. I heard that same accounting as well and, you know, the mayor and I never thought any of our boys would behave in such a disreputable manner. We must restore honor and recognition to them." Hedger had heard no such rumor but was quick to agree. For years, Maddox County had served as a convenient scapegoat.

Miss Anacelia continued, "I have a suggestion for your consideration that would restore dignity and bring distinction to both clubs. What if the FFA acts as an honor guard escorting the mayor to the bandstand and the 4-H can lead the parade." Miss Anacelia paused and quickly followed with, "And, of course, next year they could alternate roles." Grace and Hedger looked at Miss Anacelia with gratitude and relief. They had a plan. Now Hedger could devote more time to the murder mystery he was writing, and Grace was pleased with the optics of an honor guard escort for her husband, the mayor.

As Grace was leaving the Inn, she encountered Joe Cline on the porch. Joe gently reached for her hand and said, "Why, Mrs. Louden, what a pleasure to see you. I must say you look radiant this afternoon. I wonder if I might have a moment of your time. You see, I have a riverwalk proposal that might intrigue you. My Aunt Anacelia tells me you are on the board of the Bedford Landing Beautification Society." Grace visibly blushed. "Indeed, I am, Mr. Cline, and I would be delighted to learn about your proposal," thinking *He is such a handsome young man.* Unlike her husband, the mayor, Joe was tall and slender with all his hair. Grace thought he belonged on the front of a magazine.

Placing his hand at the small of her back, he asked, "Won't you join me in the dining room? I have a plan to show you." On the table, a large, detailed landscape map was spread. "Grace, I know you above all others will appreciate this concept. Imagine a riverwalk with a sculpture garden right here in Bedford Landing. It would truly be the crown jewel of Bedford Landing. Great for tourism, too!" Grace was enthralled as Joe shared the details of his proposal. "Grace, you are the heartbeat of the town, and I am confident you can rally public support." By now, Joe was holding both of her hands in his. "Joe, I have always dreamed of our very own riverwalk in Bedford Landing, but never considered a sculpture garden. What a marvelous idea."

Then in a near reverent tone, Joe said, "You know of my father Dr. Jefferson Cline? On our weekend visits to my Aunt Anacelia, he cared for poor folk in Bedford County right from this Inn. And at no cost to his patients. His death was a bitter blow to many in the community. Might I suggest we honor my father by calling the walkway the *Jefferson Cline Memorial Riverwalk?*"

*There you have it,* thought Miss Anacelia. She was seated in the parlor cringing during Joe's entire presentation. Even Peter had begun to question Joe's inexplicable zeal and long-term plans. The previous night, Miss Anacelia overheard Peter say. "Joe, do you realize we have spent *every* weekend since July away from New Orleans. This is not what we agreed. I know it is important to honor your father with the riverwalk. But every weekend? Really? And you cannot be serious about buying Haskell Crenshaw's farm at auction."

Joe calmly replied, "Serious as a heart attack."

# Bedford County Tobacco Festival

As hoped, the 2018 Bedford County Tobacco Festival was the most successful in memory. Escorted by the FFA Honor Guard, Mayor Alexander Louden stepped up to the bandstand on the courthouse lawn. Praising the town's resilience he shouted to the crowd, "When we fall down, and we surely will, we always get up, dust ourselves off, and stand tall. That is what Bedfordians do." At that, Judge Hedger Northcutt and Grace Louden stood tall from their seats on the bandstand. The crowd cheered madly.

"Now I want to make a formal announcement. The City Council has approved the erection of a riverwalk and sculpture garden right here in Bedford Landing. Many of our fine citizens have offered to donate their time and treasure to make this happen before Christmas. Special thanks must go to my lovely wife Grace and Bedford Landing's Innovator and Benefactor, Mr. Joe Cline. Step up here, Joe, so the folks can thank you." Again, the crowd cheered wildly, and a large banner was unrolled for all to see.

## *Jefferson Cline Memorial Riverwalk*
## *The Crown Jewel of Bedford Landing*

Haskell Crenshaw and his two uncles stood at the edge of the crowd. When the banner was dropped, Haskell spat on the ground and strutted away angrily to the Crenshaw Building across from the courthouse. His uncles were left again in embarrassment at Haskell's public behavior. For years the Crenshaw family struggled to gain the respectability that came so easily to the Cline family. This small scene did not escape the notice of investigative reporter Matt Conway.

The entire downtown of Bedford Landing was consumed with the festival. There was non-stop bluegrass music on the courthouse lawn with booths of local arts and crafts. Someone had located a llama who stood eating grass to the amazement of a group of small children. Someone else had brought an ostrich. Bedfordians appreciated exotic animals but looked forward mostly to the food booths. There was never a shortage of fried chicken. In recent years, there were tacos and burrito booths. However, the town's favorite was Miss Hallie's cherry pies. She always donated the proceeds to her church.

The much-anticipated Tobacco Festival Beauty Pageant preceded the parade. Sixteen-year-old Carolyn McCarty was chosen queen. Her mother Gladys had spent weeks creating her bright pink gown. Carolyn was so excited to be riding on the back of a green and white 1957 Chevrolet convertible wearing that dress and her sparkly crown.

From his upstairs office facing Main Street, Lucas Todd and Miss Anacelia had an excellent view. His hand was gently resting on her slender shoulder as they chatted throughout the parade. Miss Anacelia said, "Why, would you look at Carolyn McCarty. Used to be a rather unattractive child and now she is just beautiful." The Bedford

Landing High School Band brought up the end of the parade with their montage of "Dixie" and the "Battle Hymn of the Republic." Miss Anacelia turned her beaming face to Lucas and said, "Hedger's parade was a success." Lucas replied with a smile, "Yes, indeed. The FFA/4-H Accord held."

The planning committee saved the surprise for the last. Not to be outdone by Maddox County theatrics, a Jesse James Bank Robbery was staged. Masked bandits appeared on horses firing blanks into the air as the crowd screamed in delight. Judge Northcutt's eyes glistened. Bedford Landing was now free of the memory of the Butler legacy and their demented fan Bertha Roins.

It was not until the next morning that the lifeless body of Clayton Butler was found floating in the river. He had last been seen at the festival stumbling around the llama, his clothes disheveled, and fly undone. A sheriff's deputy drove him home.

# *Undaunted*

The town was profoundly shaken when rumors of Butler's death began to circulate the next morning. *How could it be? Once celebrated and now drunken refuse in the river.* The residents were further shocked when they opened their *Bedford Couriers*. As anticipated, the lead story was the Tobacco Festival with photos of the Jesse James Bank Robbery and Miss Carolyn McCarty wearing her sparkly crown. What they did not expect was a short story at the lower right corner of Page One headlined *Accused Kidnapper Freed*.

The news of Bertha Ronis' release did not come as a surprise to Miss Anacelia. She had received a visit from Sheriff Yaeger the week before. "Miss Anacelia, I am obligated to inform you that Bertha Roins is being released. Now we have been assured by her nephew Paul Roins she will return to Cincinnati. And I do believe we have seen the last of her but…" He paused and Miss Anacelia finished his sentence, "she still owns the house in Bedford Landing." Yaeger replied, "Yes, ma'am, she does. I think there is no danger of her returning, but it is always wise to take precautions. My deputies will keep an eye on her house over on Oak Street."

Miss Anacelia did not join the others for breakfast that morning. When Joe found her, she was seated at a table on the veranda editing the latest pages of Hedger Northcutt mystery with Cezanne resting comfortably in his chair nearby. Joe quietly asked, "Auntie A, did you see the *Bedford Courier* this morning?" Turning to Joe, she began, "You see, it is the way the law works in Kentucky. After Ms. Roins' arrest, there was a hearing where she was found to be incompetent and involuntarily committed to UK Eastern Hospital. I am told in the early days she was heavily medicated but appeared to recover her senses completely within a week to the surprise of the doctors." Miss Anacelia had her own sources of information. "The hospital was legally bound to release her after three months because it was determined she could no longer benefit from their treatment. Now here comes the mystifying part. Ms. Roins can never be held accountable for the kidnapping of little Kaylene Butler." Joe was baffled. "How is this possible, Auntie A.?" She replied. "In Kentucky, competence is non-restorative, and for this reason, Bertha Roins can never be deemed competent to stand trial for that kidnapping." Just then Lucas Todd appeared on the veranda. "Yes, son. There is an appallin' loophole in the law we mean to rectify."

It was late that evening and all the guests at the Inn had long retired. Miss Anacelia and Lucas were in her suite planning their trip to Portugal when they heard the loud, piecing bark of Cezanne. "Lucas, something is very wrong. I know it." Cezanne persisted, and then loud footsteps could be heard in the hall. "Auntie A, are you alright?" To Joe's surprise, Lucas opened the door from Miss Anacelia's suite, "Joe, Miss Anacelia is fine." Then Peter and Matt appeared in the hall followed by several other guests. Cezanne was frantically running in small circles at their feet. He stopped suddenly and threw his head back at Miss Anacelia before charging down the stairs. They all followed him through the darkened Inn to the back veranda. There they beheld Miss Anacelia's beloved gazebo, consumed in flames.

Joe gasped to see the destruction of his childhood sanctuary. It was the gazebo where he retreated from the relentless bullying of Haskell Crenshaw and his toadies. Joe searched Miss Anacelia's face as he had done so many times after the death of his parents only to see the same mix of sorrow and fury. She stood shivering in her emerald silk kimono. Her thick silver hair had come undone. Before Joe could reach her, Lucas pulled her close to him. Peter gently restrained Joe from intruding.

Transfixed by the fire, Matt Conway stood with the others on the veranda. He had returned to cover the Tobacco Festival. It was meant to be the finale to his story on the corrosive impact of celebrity worship on Bedford Landing. Now he wondered if the ending of the story was premature. *Just this morning we learned Bertha Roins was released and Clayton Butler was found dead. Now this! Why would anyone want to burn down Miss Anacelia's gazebo?* Then he recalled the behavior of Haskell Crenshaw at the Tobacco Festival and the caution of Jim Totten from the *Bedford Courier*. "Matt, don't you overlook how old rivalries might be playing into your story. We got more than one celebrity in town." Matt's musings were interrupted by the awful sound of the gazebo's collapse to the ground. Turning to the others, Matt observed Lucas Todd with his arm around Miss Anacelia. *What is Lucas doing here now? It is 1:00 in the morning!*

Miss Anacelia was lost in her own thoughts as well. She recalled her enchanted childhood shared with her older brother Jefferson. On summer nights the neighborhood children collected fireflies and ran like wild banshees across the back lawns that led down to the

Kentucky River. After games of croquet, their parents continued the party on the back veranda, drinking bourbon and sharing tales of Bedford Landing.

The children's favorite game was *Murder in The Dark*. At the beginning of the game, they gathered around that same gazebo, now in flames. Placing their sweaty little fingers into a jar they fished out a scrap of paper identifying their assigned role – Citizen, Detective, or Murderer. Rarely, did the Detective catch the Murderer before a number of Citizens were killed. Deception was key to any Murderer's success and trusting anyone was foolish. In spite of being terrified of the game, Anacelia played and was always a Citizen. One summer seven-year-old Anacelia hid in the darkness behind an ancient elm tree in mortal fear of being murdered. Then out of the darkness appeared her big brother Jefferson. He calmly approached with arms extended. "Annie, darlin'. You look so frightened. Come on over here." She fell into him and pressed her little head to his chest. Jefferson wrapped her in his arms and kindly whispered, "I am the Murderer, and you are dead." Miss Anacelia's legs gave out and she collapsed to the ground, while Jefferson went off to find his next victim.

Jefferson and Anacelia always laughed and treasured the memory of that terrifying night he murdered her in the dark.

The gazebo brought back other memories of Jefferson as well. On another cold October night in 1994, Dr. Jefferson Cline was driving his wife Cloene and their son Joe back to Frankfort. Out of the darkness, a car careened in front of them driven by an intoxicated Haskell Crenshaw. Jefferson attempted to avoid a collision. Instead, his car hit a tree killing Jefferson and Cloene instantly. Joe was left in a coma for six days with no memory of the night. Haskell and his new Porsche 911 Turbo remained intact.

No one rested the night of the gazebo fire. At first light, Sheriff Yaeger and the Fire Chief confirmed the obvious. It was arson. Joe was convinced this had to be the work of Haskell Crenshaw and it could be worse next time. Pulling Lucas aside he said, "The security system at the Inn is antiquated. We need cameras and better lighting installed! Who do you know?"

That morning Miss Anacelia sat on the veranda reflecting on the death of Clayton Butler and the release of Bertha Roins as she studied the marred landscape. The smell of the charred gazebo wafted over her. After some deliberation, Miss Anacelia concluded, Landry *will need to get the Glauber boys over here tomorrow to clean up this mess and come next spring we will build a new gazebo. Think we will place it near that willow tree.*

By mid-week a new security system was installed, and the site of the burnt gazebo cleaned and mulched. Standing in the center was a large metal sculpture purchased from one of the artists contributing to the riverwalk. It was surrounded by lemon yellow mums. Like Miss Anacelia, the Bedford Landing Inn stood proud and undaunted.

# *Crenshaw Grievance*

It was early morning a week after the Tobacco Festival when Haskell Crenshaw opened the large doors to his barn. He started the engine on the red Mercedes 380 SL and let it run for 15 minutes. He had been doing this every week since June. One of his silent partners from Mexico requested the car be hidden.

Walking back to his empty house, Haskell pondered the upcoming grand jury. His greatest liability was now dead. He smiled thinking how readily law enforcement concluded Clayton Butler got drunk and fell into the river.

Standing at the breakfast bar, Haskell prepared his morning pick-me-up of coffee, bourbon, oxycontin, and Adderall and opened the *Bedford Courier.* There was yet another front-page story about the Jefferson Cline Memorial Riverwalk. Side by side were photos of Jefferson and his son Joe. The resemblance was remarkable. Haskell scoffed. *What a self-serving son-of-a-bitch.* Then Haskell recalled the mayor's speech. "Bedford Landing's Innovator and Benefactor." *My ass!* The burnt-out gazebo brought only temporary relief from Haskell's rage.

The Cline and Crenshaws families had history. Both were landowners living in Bedford County for generations. In the darkest day of the Great Depression, hard times knocked at the Cline's door and the family was forced to sell their farm—the farm now owned by Haskell. There was only one willing buyer at the time, Horace Crenshaw. The offer was an insult and a blow to the Cline Family pride.

Not all was dark for Cline family. They were able to keep the Bedford Landing Inn and other small holdings. Over time the Clines survived the Great Depression and prospered. They were held in high esteem in Bedford County, whereas the Crenshaws became increasingly dreaded.

As the Crenshaw family wealth grew so did their sense of entitlement. Unethical business practices were overlooked, and bullying went unchallenged. More than once over the years, cases of sexual assault were dismissed as intimidated victims declined to testify. It was not until the fatal car crash in 1994 that the seemingly invincible Crenshaw family experienced accountability. This was when Haskell Crenshaw caused the death of Miss Anacelia's brother and Joe's father, Dr. Jefferson Cline.

Haskell Crenshaw initially was charged with reckless homicide. It was well established Haskell was intoxicated and driving out of control. A breathalyzer test and skid marks proved that. In Kentucky, a reckless homicide conviction generally carries one to five years in prison and $1,000 to $10,000 in fines. However, within days the charge was dropped. Haskell never spent a day in jail.

No one had high expectations for the wrongful death lawsuit brought by Joe Cline. For two years the attorneys wrangled, while Haskell publicly bullied and tormented Joe. More than once the Inn was vandalized. Then a little at a time Bedford Landing soured on the

Crenshaws in a way no bribery, bullying, or threats could change. The reckoning for the Crenshaws came two years after the crash, when their attorney recommended a settlement rather than trusting a jury from Bedford County. Every year in late October, Haskell Crenshaw felt fury over the loss of that lawsuit and every year Joe Cline felt fury over the loss of his parents to Haskell Crenshaw's drunk driving.

Haskell followed Joe Cline's successes with resentment and rancor. He attributed all his financial woes to the wrongful death lawsuit brought by Joe Cline and was convinced the substantial settlement crippled his chances for success and elevated Joe's. Haskell's wife Ruth Anne often taunted him, "Haskell, you are obsessed with that man."

Finishing his morning pick-me-up and considering another, Haskell put down the *Bedford Courier* and opened his laptop to Joe Cline's Facebook photos. Loathing himself, he scrolled to a particular photo of Joe in swim trunks. It did not take long for it to happen again. As he became more aroused, his fury grew. Standing up and adjusting his pants, he stormed out of the kitchen.

# *Community Spirit*

Grace Louden rushed to chair the Riverwalk Planning Committee. The plan called for converting a well-worn footpath along the river to a wider pea gravel walkway. It would extend from the old ferry landing downtown to Bedford Park. The walkway would be lined with gardens and strategically placed sculptures donated by local Kentucky artists. In a leap of faith, the town's website advertised the grand Riverwalk Opening at 7:00 PM on Saturday December 15, 2018. The mayor planned a speech from the bandstand exalting the Riverwalk achievement and praising the citizens of Bedford Landing.

The Butler scandal was becoming a distant memory as the new riverwalk project captivated the town of Bedford Landing. Soon the committee was overwhelmed with offers of time, talent, and treasure. A retired landscape architect from Frankfort even offered his services. Managing the volunteers proved to be overwhelming as squabbling over position and recognition surfaced.

Grace Louden called upon Miss Anacelia and began, "As you know there has been an outpouring of support for the riverwalk and we believe it will be a great success. However, some of our more enthusiastic donors seem to be competing for the limelight and we fear progress may be impeded. As you know, the mayoral election will be held in just three weeks, and I must take care to be neutral for my husband's sake." Miss Anacelia dreaded what came next. "The Riverwalk Planning Committee would greatly appreciate it if you stepped in to help."

Before returning to New Orleans for the work week, Joe had warned her, "Auntie A, you would not believe the bickering. There's the Methodists against the Baptists, the Elks versus Kiwanis. And the VFW trying to lord it over the American Legion." Even as she shook her head in dismay, Miss Anacelia bristled a bit at Joe's laughter. She loved Joe as her own son and was deeply proud of his talents. Still, the people of Bedford Landing, Kentucky were her people.

Miss Anacelia had a plan to restore order. She would host a social in the same renovated church basement that launched the Butler's *Restore My Old House*. Fliers were distributed all over town and the turnout exceeded all expectations. Refreshments were served by Landry Gelpi and the staff of the Bedford Bistro. Balloons hung from the ceiling and a large landscape map hung on the wall. With a billiard cue Joe pointed to various spots on the map fielding questions from the growing crowd around him. The excitement was building, and Grace Louden was beside herself with anticipation.

Then came a rousing speech delivered by Lucas Todd. From his years as a trial attorney, Lucas had acquired the presentation authority of an Old Testament prophet with his disheveled white hair and bushy eyebrows. The enthusiasm generated by his speech was electric.

Wearing his green eye shades. Jim Totten of the *Bedford Courier* meticulously recorded each contribution. The planning committee was surprised how many adopted entire garden spaces to honor their loved ones. Miss Anacelia herself reserved space for a small rose garden in her mother's name. *Ethella Stockton Cline 1919 to 1992.* There would be brass acknowledgement plaques.

Not in attendance at the social were the Crenshaws. However, Judge Hedger Northcutt reported later he had spotted Haskell's empty car parked across the street.

Among the donations was a check for a large garden space *In Loving Memory of John Roins 1948 to 2017*. The name of the donor went unnoticed when thank you notes were sent.

# *Fixation*

At her home in Cincinnati, Bertha Roins sank onto the old sofa she and John owned for so many years, exhausted from a Thanksgiving dinner party at the home of her nephew Paul. *This will be the last Thanksgiving I'll ever have to endure with them. I suppose it was nice enough to be invited, but how tedious and mundane the conversation was. They simply have no appreciation for public art or small-town restoration.*

*And don't tell me they didn't talk about me after I left. Wonder if Paul even told them I was found innocent.* Bertha rose from the sofa and wandered into her dreary, small kitchen to make tea, her anger rising. *I guess it is true. No good deed goes unpunished. There I was, doing the Butlers a favor. Their world was collapsing around them, and I took Kaylene to the park to distract her from the embarrassment. Did anyone express gratitude? Oh no. Of course, they didn't. Instead, I was hauled off like a common criminal.*

While waiting for the water to boil, Bertha began tugging at her hair. *The dullest... dullest little girl I ever met. But what can you expect from a family like that? I tried to help them. I really did try. Thank*

*God, my reputation was never besmirched by appearing on* Restore My Old House.

After her release from UK Eastern Hospital, Bertha began to follow Bedford Landing online and discovered Joe Cline and his riverwalk. Joe had a prominent social media presence that highlighted his many civic accomplishments in New Orleans. Bertha was engrossed researching every piece of information available. *What a remarkable, innovative young man. I am sure he has no idea who his aunt really is. All her fancy ways cannot hide what I can see. There will be consequences for her part in my unlawful arrest.*

Bertha had spent hours researching the display of public art in small-town. *I really must reach out to Joe Cline to share my thoughts.*

# A Curious Visitor

It was a bleak morning in early December. Miss Anacelia was in her suite making a leisurely start to the day while Joe and Peter quarreled in the parlor. Joe welcomed the distraction when he noticed a strange woman watching them from the front hall. She was bundled head to toe. Joe wondered how long she had had been standing there and what she had heard. Rising quickly from the settee, he asked, "May I help you, Ma'am?" Smiling demurely, she replied, "Mr. Cline, will you permit me to help you?"

As Peter retreated to the kitchen, he shot a smirk at Joe as if to say, *yet another Bedford Landing devotee…* In response, Joe discreetly managed to aim his middle finger at Peter before turning his full attention to the woman. "And to whom do I have the pleasure of meeting?"

She handed Joe her card. "Mr. Cline, my name is B. J. Roins. I am writing an article for a national periodical about small-town restoration, and I would like to profile you and your work here in this town." Joe's interest was quickened, "What periodical would that be, Ms. Roins?" Gravely she responded, "I am unable to disclose that at this time but can assure you it has a national readership."

Somewhat intrigued Joe replied, "Ms. Roins, won't you join me in the parlor. Please allow me to help you with your coat." Once she was comfortably seated, Joe offered her a glass of sherry to "take the chill off." Removing her hat and patting her hair, Bertha replied, "Why, thank you, Mr. Cline."

As they began to talk, Bertha deftly steered the conversation from her article to trends in small-town renewal and public art. Google had prepared her well for this first encounter. "Yes, Mr. Cline, I have been involved in a number of projects throughout the years. You see, it is my passion. I recently have taken a home right here in Bedford Landing. There are so many opportunities to make Bedford Landing shine, and I do look forward to contributing my considerable expertise." Joe found all of this a little improbable as she seemed to deflect whenever he asked for details. Even so, out of pure curiosity, Joe agreed to meet with her again. What harm could there be?

"Ms. Roins, regrettably I have another engagement now and we must end our visit." Bertha replied, "Mr. Cline, I thank you for your kind welcome and am confident we will become great partners." As Bertha rose from the settee, Joe placed his hand at the small of her back, coaxing her gently to the front door. Bertha quivered and felt a warm rush. At the door, Joe helped her with her coat and gave a little bow. "It has been a pleasure, Ms. Roins." He watched her toddle off to her car thinking *what a peculiar little woman. Wonder what her story really is?*

Returning home, Bertha relived every moment with Joe Cline and could barely contain her excitement for days to come. *There is a bit of an age difference, but I can tell by his touch he is attracted to me.*

Joe's "engagement" was to drive Peter to the airport in Lexington. They spoke little on the way there. As Peter grabbed his bag from the car, Joe asked, "Pick you up Friday night?" Peter did not respond and simply walked away.

# Secure the Locks

Driving back to the Inn that afternoon, Joe reflected on the quarrel. Peter questioned Joe's commitment to their relationship after the call from Grace Louden that morning. Peter could hear Joe say, "Now don't you worry, Grace. It's just a misunderstanding between two contractors. Happens all the time. I'll get it resolved. What's that? Tuesday you say?" When the call ended, Joe turned to Peter and said, "Hey, something has come up and…" Peter replied, "You are not coming to the wedding." Peter's favorite cousin Camille Honoré was to be married that Tuesday afternoon at St. Louis Cathedral. Joe, of course, was expected to accompany Peter and sit with the family.

Joe hated the distance that was growing between Peter and him and wondered, *Do I really have to be the one to make sure the riverwalk lighting is working? Maybe Peter is right. Grace is just using this as an excuse to call me.* By the time Joe returned to the Inn, he knew what needed to be done. A flight to New Orleans was booked for the following day and an apology texted for Peter to see as soon as his plane landed.

Just before dinner, Judge Northcutt showed up and joined Lucas and Joe in the parlor. In recent weeks the Judge was consumed with completing his mystery novel by New Years Day. He was so close but vexed with how Pastor Jacob Hardin could murder his wife, Mae. Then it came to him. "Lucas, it will be a laser… Yes indeed, a laser! The perfect weapon and completely untraceable. This is how it will work. Pastor Hardin hides behind a tree in the dark waiting for Mae to return home. When she reaches the curve in the road, Pastor Hardin steps out and aims the laser directly into the windshield. Mae is blinded and her car careens off the road. Then Pastor Hardin slips back home and waits for someone to report the accident." Smiling brightly, the Judge asked, "Well, what do you all think?" Before anyone could reply, Miss Anacelia announced dinner. "Won't you join us, Hedger? We set a place for you."

Landry had prepared shrimp and grits with red eye gravy. The meal was a great success, and everyone agreed it belonged on the Bistro menu. After a second glass of wine, Joe turned to Miss Anacelia, "Oh my God, Auntie A.! I forgot to tell you about my most remarkable visitor this morning. Very odd sort of woman claiming to be a journalist. Says she wants to partner with me on public art projects in Bedford Landing and do a profile for a national magazine. Has already moved here. Now what was her name? Wait a minute. I think I have her card. Yeah, here it is. *B. J. Roins, 109 Oak Street, Bedford Landing, Kentucky.*" When Joe paused to take a breath, he was met with an incredulous stare from everyone at the table. It was then he grasped what he had done. He had welcomed Bertha Roins into Miss Anacelia's parlor, spoken with her for 30 minutes, and even agreed to meet with her again.

From the kitchen, Landy Gelpi rose from the table to set the alarm and secure the locks on the Inn doors. Hedger would need to ring the bell next time.

# Decorum

The next day Bertha received no call from Joe, nor did she receive one the day following. Wondering if he misplaced her card, she called the Inn on Tuesday night and was told, "Mr. Cline has returned to New Orleans and will not return to Bedford Landing Inn until Friday evening." Bertha responded officiously, "My name is B. J. Roins. Would you please request Mr. Cline call me when he returns?" She left her number thinking, *I am sure he will want to see me as soon as he returns on Friday. Clearly, he misplaced my card or would have phoned by now.*

There was no call from Joe on Friday night. Bertha had driven by the Inn several times hoping to catch a glimpse of him. As difficult as it was, she restrained herself from calling until the next morning. "This is B. J. Roins for Joe Cline. It is urgent I speak with him immediately." The reply stunned her. "Mr. Cline received your message and is unavailable." Before she could respond, the person at the Inn ended the call. *It is clear what has happened here. Anacelia Cline wants to poison our relationship and keep us apart. She was always an interfering, spiteful woman. Joe needs to understand I was found innocent.*

Bertha drove directly to the Bedford Art Consortium, hoping to find Joe. *I will explain everything to him. Surely, he knows the Butlers were dishonest. He needs to understand they lied about the kidnapping. I was looking out for Kaylene in all that chaos. It is obvious they cooked up that story to gain sympathy. And Anacelia Cline. What a meddler! She loved the headlines and CNN coverage. Where were the headlines when I was found innocent? You can never trust the media to do the right thing.* Bertha refused to acknowledge there was no finding of innocence by the Commonwealth of Kentucky. She simply slipped through a loophole in the law.

When Bertha arrived at the Art Consortium, she was disappointed not to see Joe. What she did see was a group of attractive, young women behaving flirtatiously with the handsome salesclerk. *Would you look at those foolish girls and how they are dressed. They do not have the first idea how to behave with decorum. I am sure Joe would find them most unappealing. He appreciates the depth and life experience only a more mature woman can bring.* That day Bertha wore a sensible grey trench coat that nearly reached the floor. The broad brim of her darker grey felt hat was turned down on all sides to protect her from the elements.

Bertha began strolling through the gallery. She was intrigued by the large-scale contemporary pieces, and she began to envision how Joe might invite her to accompany him in acquiring others. *Who knows where our travels might lead. I should apply for a passport.*

Bertha's fantasy was interrupted by annoyingly loud giggles. *Simply unacceptable behavior,* she thought glaring in disdain at the salesclerk and his gaggle of girls. *I will certainly share this experience with Joe.* Bertha moved to the next piece. It was a grotesque abstract of a mushroom with the face of an old woman peaking from the cap and fingers protruding from the stalk. Bertha emitted her own giggle and then gasped when she realized the abstract was her own reflection in a full-length mirror.

There was more laughter and Bertha was convinced it was directed at her. She rushed from the gallery and headed to a mall outside Frankfort.

# Bombshell at the Bistro

It was a bustling Saturday night at the Bedford Bistro. Haskell Crenshaw sat alone at the bar. He could hear raucous laughter from a table in the back, but a large plant blocked his view.

At 8:30, Bertha Roins entered the Bistro wearing her new gold and black animal print top with black leggings. Her hair was dyed a burgundy color and her lipstick bright red. Approaching the bar, she imagined how Joe would welcome her with a glass of sherry. He just needed to understand how appallingly she had been treated by law enforcement and the media. Bertha could almost feel the warmth of his hand guiding her to a small private table in the back. After taking a seat, she became aware of the laughter and recognized Joe's voice. Joe was entertaining Peter Honoré and Matt Conway with stories of his misadventures in New Orleans.

When the laughter subsided, Matt Conway spoke with great solemnity. "So, Joe, I hear you had a distinguished visitor." In equal formality, Joe responded, "I did indeed. Last Sunday morning, a woman of some years and girth appeared in the front hall purporting to be a journalist for a periodical of national repute. She wanted to interview me about the Riverwalk. After we were seated in the parlor, her story shifted. She tells me she has moved to Bedford Landing with a plan to contribute her *considerable* expertise bringing art to small towns." Matt Conway exclaimed, "Is there no end to this woman's delusions?" and Peter interjected, "And she tells Joe she plans to be his partner." Smiling at Peter, Joe continued. "At dinner that evening I shared the story of my very curious visitor and when I finished, there was complete silence at the table. It was only then I realized the odd little woman was none other than the lunatic Bertha Roins." With that, laughter erupted from the table.

Haskell became strangely aware of Bertha's stiffening body and saw her contorted face reflected in the mirror behind the bar. When she pushed back the bar stool, there was a loud screeching sound on the floor. Inside Bertha's head there was the sound of a freight train raging. She marched back to the noisy table and was stunned to see Joe lightly kissing Peter on the lips. Without a single word, Bertha grabbed a glass from the table and threw the contents into Joe's astonished face. Returning to the bar, she fumbled to collect her bag causing the large plant to crash to the floor. There was only muffled laughter as Bertha resolutely strode from the Bistro into her own darkness.

Haskell remained for another hour gleaning whatever he could from the conversation in the back. The voices of the three men were quieter now. Joe was beginning to have qualms about his cruel mockery and said, "She is such a pathetic creature. You know Landry Gelpi spotted her driving by the Inn several times last week, and I have been avoiding her calls. After tonight I imagine we've seen the last of her." Matt cautioned, "Joe. I am not so certain." Peter who had not yet made the shift in tone interjected, "Oh My God! Did you see the way she was dressed and what was up with that hair? Honestly,

Joe, what did you do to lead her on?" Matt gravely responded, "For a woman like Bertha Roins, it would take little. She likely has a condition called erotomania." Peter's eyes widened, "What's that. Matt?" Pausing briefly for dramatic effect, Matt continued, "Erotomania is a delusion in which a person believes that another person is in love with them. They may have never even met. This disorder can lead to harassment, stalking, and even worse. Not dissimilar was the celebrity worship Bertha Roins had for the Butlers last summer that sent her to the nuthouse. This woman could be dangerous, Joe, and you need to keep an eye out!"

When they returned to the Inn, Lucas Todd and Miss Anacelia shared Matt's assessment of the danger. Miss Anacelia recalled how Kaylene Butler dangled from the swing at Waveland Park as Bertha recklessly pushed it higher and higher. It was decided for Joe's safety and the good of the Inn a restraining order would be prudent.

Haskell Crenshaw made his own decision that night. *Bertha Roins would be the perfect instrument.*

# *Grooming*

He awoke to his cell phone blaring the soundtrack from the *Psycho shower scene*. It was Ruth Anne again calling about child support. "Jesus Christ, will that woman ever let up?" It had been ten months since his last payment, and her attorneys were threatening further action.

Haskell was heavily in debt and needed someone to blame. His farm was in foreclosure and his attorneys had formally withdrawn due nonpayment. It seemed no credible attorney would agree to represent him, and the grand jury was convening in January.

He began to ruminate again how the wrongful death lawsuit had given Joe Cline an unfair advantage in life. *My car may have swerved slightly into his lane, but it was Jefferson Cline who panicked and ran into that tree. He was the cause of his own death.* The phone blared again, and he put it in silent mode.

For weeks Haskell had pondered how to humiliate Joe Cline by disrupting the opening of his beloved Jefferson Cline Memorial Riverwalk. His minions would no longer do his bidding after the gazebo fire. Like his attorneys, they too turned their backs on him for non-payment. However, Bertha Roins arrived just in time, and he would use all his guile to weaponize her.

Bertha remained in bed until Monday morning after the incident at the Bedford Bistro. Staring at the ceiling she contemplated her next move. *The Clines must be punished.*

It was late afternoon on Monday when Bertha opened her door to Sheriff Harlan Yaeger. "Ms. Roins, I am here to deliver this restraining order issued by Judge John Heilman in reference to Mr. Joe Cline. This is the second restraining order you have received this year here in Bedford Landing. I suggest you take heed, Ms. Roins. Bedford Landing is a quiet town, and we plan to keep it that way." Bertha stared at the Sheriff in disbelief. She grabbed the document and slammed the door in the Sheriff's face.

> This **CEASE AND DESIST ORDER** demands that you immediately discontinue and do not at any point in the future under any circumstances do the following to Joe Cline: speak to, contact, pursue, harass, attack, strike, bump into, brush up against, push, tap, grab, hold, threaten, telephone (via cellular or landline), instant message, page, fax, email, follow, stalk, shadow, disturb his peace, keep him under surveillance, gather information about and/or block his movements at home, work, social gatherings or religious functions.

Not long after Sheriff Yaeger departed, the doorbell rang again. In fury, Bertha threw open the door and shouted, "What?" Standing before her was a tall, gaunt man with thinning red hair. He held a large bouquet of roses and bowed. "Ms. Roins, please permit me to introduce myself and offer to you these lovely flowers. I am Haskell Crenshaw and on behalf of the entire Crenshaw family I extend our most heartfelt sympathy for the abysmal treatment you have received here in Bedford Landing at the hands of the Cline family." Bertha's eyes narrowed briefly as she awkwardly took the bouquet. "Ms. Roins, I too have suffered from egregious treatment by the Clines and understand the pain you may be feeling now." Bertha's curiosity overcame her suspicion. "Mr. Crenshaw, I do not make it a practice of inviting strange men into my home, but under the circumstances may I offer you a cup of tea?" "It would be my honor to take tea with you, Ms. Roins."

Haskell spent nearly two hours grooming Bertha. He listened carefully to her grievances and delusions of grandeur. By the time he left, she had shared her entire life story much of which was fabricated. Haskell stroked her wounded ego and assured her that someday Bedford Landing would come to appreciate her considerable expertise in small-town renewal. "Joe Cline cannot hold a candle to what you have to offer." To which she replied, "Mr. Crenshaw, I tried to help in my own way but now I know him to be a charlatan and headline hunter as is his aunt Anacelia Cline." Haskell could tell he was making progress. "It is a crime the way the Clines have run roughshod over my family and this town. Something needs to be done to expose them for what they are." They agreed to meet again. Driving home, Haskell thought, *this woman is a total nut job.*

They met several times that week and by Thursday a plan was hatched. They knew Mayor Louden was to deliver his speech from the bandstand at exactly 7:00 on Saturday night. Across the street from a second-floor window in the Crenshaw Building, Bertha would use a bullhorn to drown out Mayor Louden's speech with her own. She envisioned the crowd enraptured with her vision for Bedford Landing and turning away from the mayor and Joe Cline. Haskell expected another result. The crowd would be reduced to laughter at the competing bombast. He could always claim later to be duped by a deranged woman for whom he felt pity. They agreed to meet on Friday afternoon at the Crenshaw Building. Bertha would need to know how to get into the building unseen and from which upper room window she would deliver the speech. Bertha could hardly wait. She already had the bullhorn.

On Friday morning, Bertha sat at Bedford Park overlooking the Riverwalk, meticulously crafting her speech. *I was always recognized as an excellent orator in high school. All those wasted years married to John Roins.* When she saw Miss Anacelia below placing the remaining brass acknowledgement plaques, Bertha cackled. One plaque was placed in the garden space reserved for Bertha's late husband John Roins.

That afternoon Bertha arrived at the Crenshaw Building at 4:00 pm as they agreed. Standing in the building's outer hall, she was surprised to find the door to the offices locked and the lights out. Bertha banged on the door. A janitor mopping the outer hall floor called to her, "Ain't nobody there, Ma'am. On Fridays, they close up by 3:00." Bertha glared at him and pounded on the door again shouting "Haskell, I am here. Haskell, open the door." The janitor shook his head and said, "Ma'am, you best be leavin' now. We gonna' lock up the entire building pretty soon. You don't wanna' get stuck in here." Bertha jerked her chin and reached for her cell phone angrily punching Haskell's number. It went straight to voicemail. Bertha's face turned a dark red as she stormed from the building.

# Anticipation and Dread

The night before the Riverwalk Opening, Miss Anacelia hosted a celebratory dinner. Mayor Louden and his wife Grace were among the guests. As they approached the Inn, Grace enthused, "Miss Anacelia has outdone herself this year for Christmas. The Inn is positively shimmering. We must be sure to have our tourism website updated with holiday photos of the Inn." Removing all references to the Butlers Family and *Restore This Old House* had left a large gap.

Miss Anacelia greeted the Loudens at the door and invited them to the parlor where Lucas Todd had been regaling the other guests with stories of his courtroom victories and near fiascos. Judge Northcutt contributed some of his own. Miss Anacelia placed her hand on Lucas' shoulder, "Pardon me, Lucas. Let us welcome the Mayor and Mrs. Louden to our small group." The men stood until Grace was seated by the fire. She glowed from the warmth of the fire and their attention. Before Lucas could resume his tale, Landry Gelpi appeared with champagne cocktails.

Landry and Peter worked from early morning preparing the meal. No one was allowed in the kitchen while they labored. The meal was to be a triumph and it was.

## MENU

*\* First Course\**
Port Poached Pear

*\*Second Course\**
Lobster Onion Bisque

*\*Entrees Course\**
Duck Breast
*Long Grain Wild Rice, Sugar Snap Peas, Plum Sauce*

*\*Dessert\**
Creole Bread Pudding

After everyone was seated, Matt could not contain himself, "Mayor, have you heard anything about the grand jury coming up next month." This was not a subject the mayor nor anyone else wanted to discuss that night. Lucas dug his shoe deeply into Matt's ankle and steered the conversation to the meal. "Miss Anacelia, I believe there could be no restaurant in all of New Orleans to equal this meal. Peter beamed while Landy Gelpi took his seat at the breakfast table and poured another glass of Côte du Rhone. He loved reflecting on his work in the quiet of the kitchen.

Before dessert was served, Mayor Louden stood and held his glass high, "Ladies and gentlemen, may I toast our gracious hostess Miss Anacelia Cline and her dynamic nephew Joe who have given heart and soul to our town." Joe profusely thanked everyone, especially Grace Louden. "It has been an honor to partner with Grace and I can only look forward to our future endeavors." There was applause across the table. Lucas carefully watched Miss Anacelia smile, her hands held tightly in her lap. Earlier she whispered to him, "Lucas I have this feeling something is off."

In her home only blocks away, Bertha paced from one room to the next pulling at her hair. *Where can he be and why is he not answering my calls. I will not be ignored.*

# Betrayal

After his own fitful night, Haskell awoke the next morning in deep paranoia. His world was imploding. The previous morning his two uncles summoned him to their offices at Crenshaw Enterprises. "Son, we have done everything we can to support you over the years, but it is time you take full responsibility for your actions. This morning the board voted to discontinue all association with you. We were able to get them to agree not to press the embezzlement charges, but you can expect no severance package. You are now *persona non grata* at Crenshaw Enterprises."

However, it was the call from his more determined creditors that sent Haskell reeling. He was warned failure to pay his debt by the upcoming Monday would lead to his end. "Times's up, Haskell." For some time, Haskell knew this day would come and he had planned for it. He opened an overseas account with money embezzled from Crenshaw Enterprises and his money laundering operation with the Butlers. His plan now was to slip out of town in the red Mercedes. When he opened the trunk, he was surprised to discover two duffle bags containing easily over a million dollars. Haskell surmised it was untraceable cash intended for Butler Enterprises. The FBI raid in

July had prevented delivery and the cash smuggler never returned to collect it. Haskell assumed she was likely dead. His anxiety was slightly abating, but he knew he must rush.

While Haskell was packing, Bertha set off in her Ford Focus for his farmhouse. She had some difficulty locating it and had become increasingly exasperated at each wrong turn. Her calls to Haskell still were going straight to voicemail. *Haskell had better have a good excuse for abandoning me.* She recalled her visit to the Crenshaw Building the day before. *I could hear the janitor snickering as I left.* Bertha could not tolerate ridicule. At the memory, she began pulling at her hair and scratching at her face. Then the entrance to the Haskell farmhouse appeared. *No hiding from me.*

The steps to the farmhouse porch were icy and some were broken. Bertha nearly fell. At the front door, she called out for Haskell repeatedly ringing the doorbell. There was no response, and she began to bang on the door. After some time, she stepped down the treacherous steps and marched to the back of the house where she encountered Haskell stuffing bags in the backseat of a red Mercedes. Haskell did not look up or even bother to acknowledge her. *How dare he dismiss me,* she thought.

Legs apart and hands on her hips, Bertha demanded to know. "What on earth are you doing and why are you avoiding me? I will NOT be ignored. We have a plan." Haskell had two pick-me-ups that morning and looked at her with fire in his eyes. "Plan?? I have no idea what you are talking about, Ms. Roins. All I know is you are a town joke. Everyone is talking about how you were dressed and how you acted at the Bistro last Saturday night. They are calling you *Bertha, the Bedford Bistro Bombshell,* don't you know." Bertha's face had turned nearly purple with rage.

"Ms. Bombshell, are you having another one of your delusions?" With that he turned his back and broke into his high-pitched laugh. Bertha was no fool. She recognized "gaslighting" when she heard it.

Without a second thought, Bertha picked up a tire iron from the open trunk and bludgeoned Haskell to death. It was then she recognized the long, deep scratch on the driver's door of the red Mercedes. Bertha bashed in all the windows and serenely drove back to her home on Oak Street.

# Lest We Ever Forget

Night had fallen. Bertha sat in her car at Bedford Park clutching the bullhorn. *One's plans must be flexible in the face of adversity. This is a far better venue to deliver my speech. The lighting was very poor at the Crenshaw Building.* Her new plan was to stand at the park's edge illuminated by the brights of her Ford Focus and deliver her speech to the strollers below.

*I cannot wait for the news tomorrow. The Clines will be so humiliated, and I shall be praised for my vision and good judgement.* Then recalling the death of her husband at Sunset Cliffs, she erupted in giggles. *I must be certain not to fall like poor John. He was such a fool.* She giggled again. The anticipation was making Bertha giddy. She felt an urgent need to go to the bathroom but that would have to wait.

Across town at the Bedford Bistro, Joe Cline and his delegation had gathered for drinks waiting for the mayor's speech to begin. Joe, Peter, and Matt were all talking at once as Lucas and Miss Anacelia watched in some amusement. Then they heard the ringing of Bedford Landing's own Liberty Bell. Joe proudly led the group from the Bistro to the courthouse lawn where they encountered a celebration already in progress. From the bandstand Bedford County's own bluegrass quintet played Christmas songs as old friends greeted one another heartily. Most had known each other since childhood. Old men exchanged flasks conducting their own private bourbon tasting while children whispered their requests to Santa Claus. Joe was pleased to see how warmly Miss Anacelia was greeted by everyone.

As the quintet completed their final song "God Rest Ye Merry Gentlemen," Mayor Louden and his wife ascended the bandstand. The town was riveted by Mayor Louden's speech. He spoke at length about the proud history of their town and praised the citizens of Bedford Landing for maintaining that legacy. "Although special recognition should go to my tenacious wife Grace and that fine gentleman from New Orleans, Mr. Joe Cline, it is the citizens of Bedford Landing who truly met the Riverwalk challenge overcoming any adversity with good cheer. We stand here this evenin' as a testament to your unconquerable spirit." The people cheered wildly until Mayor Louden held up his palms. When they had fallen silent, he continued in a more sober tone, "I have just one final thing to say to you all. Lest we ever forget, there is one more person to acknowledge. We are here tonight to honor Dr. Jefferson Cline, who tirelessly treated the citizens of Bedford County at no cost. It is in his name that we open the Jefferson Cline Memorial Riverwalk. May I wish you all a Merry Christmas. God Bless the Commonwealth of Kentucky and the United States of America." Tears were streaming down Miss Anacelia's face. The mayor shouted, "Let there be light." A switch was flipped, and the Riverwalk lights shone brightly as the choir from the Bedford Landing Baptist Church lifted their voices to belt out "Joy to the World."

Grace Louden rushed from the bandstand pushing Peter aside to take Joe's arm as they led the promenade down to the Riverwalk.

Miss Anacelia and Lucas followed, while Peter rolled his eyes and took a step back to walk with Landry Gelpi. Matt Conway could be seen taking photos from the bandstand with Jim Totten of *The Bedford Courier*.

The Riverwalk was truly magical that evening. The illuminated sculptures stood like angels guiding the way while carolers dressed in Victorian garb sang holiday favorites. Grace Louden was euphoric. She could not contain herself and kissed Joe on both cheeks. "Joe Cline, this is one of the most thrilling nights of my life."

Miss Anacelia paused at the garden space dedicated to her mother Ethella, and Lucas stepped back to allow her that moment. To no one in particular, she said, "Mama always favored yellow roses. We will plant come Spring."

Judge Hedger Northcutt was excitedly weaving his way through the promenade. Making his way to the front, he boldly declared, "This will be a night no one will ever forget in Bedford Landing."

From her perch at Bedford Park, Bertha could hear the voices of the carolers approaching. The time had come. Turning on the interior lights, she hurriedly patted her burgundy-colored hair and reapplied the bright red lipstick. *I am camera ready now. After tonight Bedford Landing will hail me as the town's innovator and the Clines will be exposed as common publicity seekers.*

Just then Bertha was stunned to hear sirens blaring and see flashing red and blue lights heading toward the park. *Oh my God. They found Haskell Crenshaw.* She felt a terrific pain tear through her brain. Brutal memories of her rejection and humiliation in Bedford Landing consumed her. *I will not endure one more indignity.* Turning the wheel of her car Bertha headed down the utility road to the Riverwalk. There she saw the walkers approaching at a distance. Without hesitation, she slammed the accelerator to the floor. The little car lunged forward and barreled erratically toward the walkers knocking over a sculpture and ripping into the power box. To everyone's horror, the Riverwalk went completely dark. Only the interior lights of her oncoming car could be seen.

There were shrieks and screams as terrified walkers ran for their lives into the pitch. One child almost rolled into the icy river but was blocked by a large landscape stone. Grace Louden twisted her ankle and fell into Joe knocking them both down. Lucas and Miss Anacelia had stepped from the walkway when they heard wailing from a terrified little boy separated from his parents. Within seconds Miss Anacelia gathered him in her arms and brought him to safety.

Then out of the darkness, a small, round figure emerged on the walkway. He pointed a laser directly into the windshield of the oncoming car. Thinking the light was from local television news cameras Bertha gave a grand smile before her car cruelly plunged into the dark frigid waters of the Kentucky River. The figure with the laser disappeared into the chaos of the crowd and was never identified.

# Discovery

The following day there was a heavy snowfall, and the Ford Focus was not hauled from the icy river until late afternoon. Sheriff Harlan Yaeger's first thought was, *Thank God it was Bertha Roins and not some knucklehead from Maddox County.* During Mayor Louden's speech the previous night, a rumor was spreading that a Maddox County boy planned to ambush the strollers with a paintball gun when they reached the park. The Sheriff dispatched his deputies, but they were too late to avert the calamity.

No one in Bedford Landing had an appetite for the national attention this incident could garner. The Butlers had done enough damage. The sheriff's office formally attributed the near catastrophe to reckless driving by a confused old woman, although Miss Anacelia and others from the Inn knew better. This was an attempt at mass murder by the erotomaniac Bertha Roins. She had publicly humiliated herself in pursuit of Joe Cline and could not bear his rejection and the town mockery. Her driving was indeed reckless but her intentions clear. On that frigid December night at the Riverwalk Opening, Bertha Roins attempted to plow into the citizens of Bedford Landing. There were varying reports of a green light flashing in the dark but were never substantiated and soon forgotten.

Just as Sheriff Yaeger was finishing the paperwork on the "accident," the 911 call came. A young UPS driver delivering packages to the Crenshaw farmhouse found the snow-covered body of Haskell Crenshaw by the barn. Feral pigs were gnawing at Haskell's head. This was the driver's first day on the job.

A week passed when Sheriff Yaeger and Lucas Todd met at their favorite tavern just outside of town. Sheriff Yaeger spoke first. "Well, Lucas, we turned the investigation over to the Kentucky State Police. Bedford County just doesn't have the resources to handle a case like this." Lucas sipped his bourbon and waited for more to be shared. "We don't exactly know how long Haskell was out there like that. It was a God-awful mess, and the crime scene was contaminated by the pigs. You know about the pigs, right?" Lucas nodded solemnly, staring into his nearly empty glass. As a medic in Vietnam, Lucas had seen his own share of gruesome sights. The Sheriff continued, "There was this red Mercedes with Haskell's SUV plates. The windows were all bashed and the backseat full of Haskell's bags. Funny, the trunk was open and completely empty. We found his passport sitting right out on the dashboard. Looked like ole Haskell was absconding from his creditors and the grand jury." Then he paused and abruptly ended the account, "Well, guess it's not my problem now." Lucas replied, "Harlan, you did the right thing calling in the State Police. Haskell Crenshaw was tangled up with so many messes you could waste your entire career investigating him."

After another round Lucas asked brightly, "Coming to Miss Anacelia's Open House on New Years Day? Landry will be making his famous Hoppin' Johns, and you know how much Miss Anacelia

Roaming Feral Pigs at Crenshaw Farm

looks forward to seeing you all." Then as an afterthought Lucas said, "Oh, remember Audrey Wilcox? She'll be there. Ran into some family trouble back in Kansas City. Looks as if she will be staying at the Inn. Hopes to start law school in Lexington come September. I always thought she was a smart girl. Just needed to find her way."

# *Media Sensation*

It was late August 2019. Across Bedford Landing, folks were tuning into *CBS Sunday Morning* to see one of Bedford Landing's most esteemed citizens, Judge Hedger Northcutt. His murder mystery was published in the Spring and had become a bestseller. At Bedford Landing Inn, a large television screen was set up on the veranda. Landry Gelpi, with the help of Audrey Wilcox, served Bloody Marys to the guests.

Joe and Peter were amusing everyone with their own tales of Bedford Landing and the new riverboat project. Mayor Louden and wife Grace beamed as they were convinced the riverboat would bring prosperity to the town and be their ticket to the statehouse. To the mayor's relief, the grand jury was suspended after Clayton Butler and Haskell Crenshaw turned up dead. Many in Bedford County shared the mayor's sentiments.

As Joe was about to share the complexities of Kentucky gambling regulations, Miss Anacelia rang a small silver bell. "It's time everybody. Landry, would you kindly turn up the volume?" They all watched in awe as Judge Northcutt spoke proudly of his town. The cameras

Susan DuVall

followed him as he strolled across the Bedford County Courthouse lawn down to the Jefferson Cline Memorial Riverwalk. Looking out at the river, Judge Northcutt declared, "I do not believe there could be a finer town in all of Kentucky than Bedford Landing."

The camera then switched to an in-studio interview with Jane Pauley who would be the first of several morning show hosts to invite the Judge. "Welcome to our show, Judge Northcutt." Nodding his head deferentially. Northcutt replied, "Why it is my pleasure to be here, Ms. Pauley." After some initial chitchat Pauley inquired, "Judge, you must know what is on the mind of many of our viewers. Are the characters in your book based on real people? For instance, tell us about the elderly woman who becomes an unhinged stalker. Where did that come from? Judge Northcutt briefly studied his hands and then with a broad smile answered. "Well, you know, Ms. Pauley. Let me put it this way. Writing my story brings to mind my years on the bench. I was presented with truths, half-truths, and outright lies. Sometimes hard to discern when one ends and the other starts."

When the interview was concluded, Miss Anacelia looked out at her new gazebo, the sculpture, and to the river beyond. "Landry, would you please refresh everyone's drink? We must make a toast to Hedger for his fine accomplishment."

No one ever figured Judger Hedger Northcutt to wind up a media sensation.

## *The End*

# Acknowledgements

I would like to express my gratitude.

My most excellent friend Cynthia Weadock walked every step with me as this story unfolded and characters emerged. Her enthusiasm, endless ideas, and humor have made this journey incredibly fun.

Maria Hackett created the interior illustrations that perfectly portrayed the soul of the story and its place in time. It was a pleasure to collaborate with Maria.

K.J. Wetherholt was my editor, consultant, and mentor. Her insight, guidance and encouragement were an inspiration.

# About the Author

Susan DuVall was born a Kentuckian and has remained one in her heart no matter where her life has led. Her magical childhood was spent in a small river town where the cultural richness, haunting tales, and very peculiar characters intrigued her and never faded from memory.

Susan became a mother, technology professional, world traveler, writer, and ardent admirer of dachshunds. She lives in Tucson, Arizona with her long-haired dachshund Henri Matisse DuVall.